Step-Chain

All over the country children go to stay with step-parents, stepbrothers and stepsisters at the weekends. It's just like an endless chain. A step-chain. *Secrets and Lies* is the ninth link in this step-chain.

I'm Katie, and I'm intrigued by a photo I've found hidden in my brother's room. I can't understand why Matt is so cross with me when I ask him about it – until I learn the truth. My family is more complicated than I thought. But Mum would be devastated if she knew what we were doing. So we end up telling lies. Then even more lies. And soon the secret gets too big . . .

Collect the links in the step-chain! You never know who you'll meet on the way . . .

Step-Chain

SECRETS AND LIES

Ann Bryant

First published in Great Britain 2002
by Egmont Books Limited
239 Kensington High Street
London W8 6SA

Series editor: Anne Finnis

ISBN 1 4052 0261 0

1 3 5 7 9 10 8 6 4 2

Typeset by Avon DataSet Ltd, Bidford on Avon, B50 4JH
(www.avondataset.co.uk)
Printed and bound in Great Britain by
Cox & Wyman Ltd, Reading, Berkshire

CONTENTS

Step-Chain

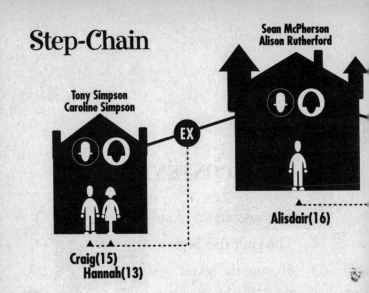

Sean McPherson
Alison Rutherford

Tony Simpson
Caroline Simpson

EX

Alisdair(16)

Craig(15)
Hannah(13)

Martin Marchant & Dawn Willis

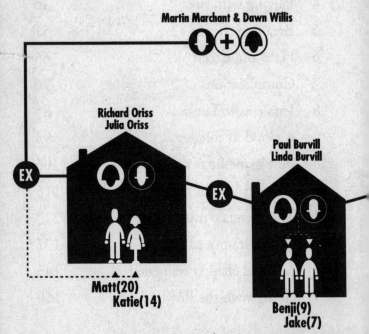

Richard Oriss
Julia Oriss

Paul Burvill
Linda Burvill

EX

EX

Matt(20)
Katie(14)

Benji(9)
Jake(7)

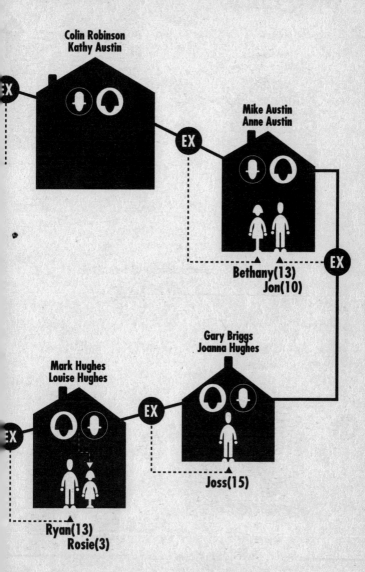

Read on to discover all the links . . .

1 THE MYSTERIOUS PHOTOGRAPH

Oh *great*. Not another battery. What is wrong with this personal CD player? Maybe it's not a CD player at all. Maybe it's a serial battery killer in disguise. I thought about calling downstairs to ask Mum if we've got any spares, but I know we haven't. Unless . . . That's a point. Maybe Matt's got some hidden away somewhere.

My brother Matt is away at university, so it is actually possible to get into his room without tripping over anything or having to hold your breath and tiptoe carefully among the decaying socks.

Good plan, Katie. Go for it!

I rummaged through his desk drawers, starting at the top and working my way down. What is it about boys? Even when they're really ancient – well, twenty seems pretty ancient to me – they don't mind living in a mess. They chuck things all over the place. How do they ever find anything?

And then my hand came out of the bottom drawer holding a photo. I glanced at it. A man and a woman with their arms round each other smiled up at me. With them was a girl who looked a bit younger than me. I put it back in the drawer. I didn't know these people. But hang on – there was something familiar about the girl.

I took the photo into the light and looked at it more carefully. I guessed they were a family, though the parents looked quite young. Mind you, that's only because our parents are older. But what was Matt keeping their picture in his desk for? That's not like him.

'Katie!' Mum's voice floated up the stairs. 'It's ready.'

'Coming!'

I dropped the photo back in the drawer again and galloped downstairs. It wasn't that much of a mystery, after all. I mean, Matt meets all sorts of people that I know nothing about, doesn't he? And it was probably no big deal that the girl looked a bit familiar. After all, loads of people look like other people, don't they?

The moment we sat down to eat, the phone rang. It was my friend Chloe, from school. She wanted to know what answers I'd got for the maths homework.

'Sorry, Chlo, haven't done it yet.'

'Haven't done it?' hissed Mum.

'What have you been doing up there, then?' whispered Dad.

But they didn't really need the answer to

that question. Even if they knew I'd spent the last hour reading this really good book about star signs with my telly on in the background, it wouldn't bug them in the slightest. I don't get grief from my parents. They're not like that. They trust me to get my homework done and hand it in on time, so I always make sure I do. That's how it works, this trust thing. All my friends say I'm so lucky to have such lovely, reasonable parents. And my friends are right. I *am* lucky.

But there's something about my parents that only Chloe, my best friend, knows. You see, my dad isn't really my dad. I've always called him Dad because he's the only dad I've ever known. My real dad left Mum for another woman called Dawn when I was just a baby and Matt was six, and Mum was so devastated she refused to have anything more to do with him. She wouldn't let him see me ever again. I don't expect he was bothered about that. He can't have been, or he wouldn't have left me. Over the years I've picked up that he sometimes got drunk and that this Dawn woman was much younger than him. No wonder Mum was so upset.

Apparently Matt wanted to see his daddy though, so Mum put up with the odd visit, but that soon faded out when Richard, our lovely new dad, appeared on the scene. He and Mum got married within a year of meeting each other, and they've been madly in love ever since. And I mean *madly in love*! I'm not kidding, I have to tell my friends to close their mouths and stop staring sometimes, because they've never seen two people as old as my parents who still hold hands in public. Every time Chloe and Mia purse their lips to tell me *They're so sweeeeeeet!* I feel totally embarrassed about it.

So I had a quick chat with Chloe on the phone, then after we'd finished eating, Dad told me to bring the maths downstairs.

'Let me give you a hand with it,' he said, giving me his 'kind' look as I call it.

Actually, he always looks kind. That's because he *is* kind. There's absolutely nothing he wouldn't do for me. Poor old Dad didn't have a clue how to do the maths, but by the time I'd explained it to him and done the first question to give him an example, I realised it was quite easy, and I rattled through the rest.

'There, darling,' beamed Mum, putting one arm round me and one round Dad. 'Aren't you lucky to have a dad who understands all this complicated stuff!'

I couldn't believe what I was hearing. 'But *I* did it!'

Mum laughed. 'Yes, but you wouldn't have if it hadn't been for Dad, would you?'

I was about to protest again, when I realised it was actually true. I gave them both an exasperated look, which just made them laugh, then said I was going up to my room to watch telly.

It was one of my favourite programmes, but after a bit I realised I just wasn't concentrating. My mind kept drifting back to that photo. I went to get it out of Matt's desk drawer, then sat on my own bed and had a good look. It was no big deal really. In fact I didn't know why I was so interested. It was just a photo of some people Matt knew. Or maybe he didn't know them any more. In fact he probably didn't even remember he'd got this photo in his drawer. I looked closely at the girl's face. It *was* a bit familiar, and that was what bugged me.

Well, there was an easy way to solve the mystery – text Matt.

I got my mobile and tapped in *Looking for battery in your room. Found photo. Man, woman, girl. Who are they?*

His reply came almost immediately – *Just some people I met. How's tricks?*

Fine. What people? I replied.

And five minutes later he actually rang my mobile.

'Listen, Katie, that photo you found . . .'

I *knew* there was going to be something intriguing about it. I just *knew*.

'Yeah?'

'Well, the thing is, don't mention it to Mum and Dad, will you?' Through my mind buzzed about ten reasons why I wasn't allowed to mention it. I'd got as far as Matt being a secret agent for a dangerous underground organisation, and these people being the enemy in *big* disguise, when he brought me back to the here and now, his voice all worried and breathy. 'Oh God, you haven't shown Mum already, have you?'

'No, course not.' I held the phone really close to my mouth and spoke quietly, my heart beating faster than usual. 'So who are they?'

'It doesn't matter. It's nothing to do with

you. I just don't want Mum and Dad to know, that's all.' He sounded snappy and urgent now.

'Oh, come on, Matt. You've got me all curious. That's so unfair. You've got to tell me now. I won't tell Mum and Dad, honestly.' There was a pause. I thought he was cracking. 'OK, I won't tell *anyone.*'

He still didn't answer immediately, but I could hear his brain ticking over. 'Look, I'll be home at the weekend and I'll explain it all then.'

'Oh, cool! I didn't know you were coming home this weekend!'

His voice went flat. 'I wasn't, but I am now.'

Specially because of this . . .

'That's two more days! I'll die of curiosity before then.'

'Well, you'll have to die.'

'I don't get what the big secret is –'

'And keep your mouth shut, OK?'

My bedroom door opened. 'What secret?'

said Mum, smiling like an excited child. 'Is it Matt? Has he got a secret? Is it good news?'

She was reaching for the phone. 'Mum's just come in, Matt. She wants to talk to you,' I said in my most normal voice. I had to give Matt the chance to think of something. I spoke as lightly as I could. 'She wants to know what the big secret is.'

I handed Mum the phone, feeling a bit guilty. I'd put Matt on the spot and I hadn't meant to do that.

Mum was smiling into the mouthpiece – she so adores Matt. 'Uh-huh,' she was saying as she went out of my room. Goodness knows what 'secret' Matt came up with, but it was obviously doing the trick because I didn't hear Mum fall downstairs or break into hysterical wails or anything.

2 THE GUILT TRIP BEGINS

I don't know how I got through the next two days. I'd promised Matt I wouldn't say anything to anyone about the photo, so I thought I'd better not even mention it to Chloe at school. I just had to sit tight and wait for him to come home and explain. I've always kept promises and I hardly ever tell lies. My friends think I'm a bit weird like that, but it's just the way I am. I suppose it's to do with my upbringing.

Chloe wanted me to go over to her place on Friday night.

'The thing is, Chlo, Matt's coming home.'

'But you'll see him for the rest of the weekend,' she said, all wide-eyed and sad.

So then I felt horrible and mean. 'I haven't seen him for ages, you see.'

'I think it's brilliant that your family's such a *family* family!' said Mia.

(We knew what she meant.)

'You'll come into town on Saturday though, won't you?' said Chloe.

'Yeah, course.'

On Friday evening I spent ages changing in and out of loads of clothes. I know he's only my brother, but he's really cool and I want him to be proud of me. I must seem so young to him, so the older I can make myself look, the better. I've only got a bit of make-up, but I laid it on as thickly as possible and thought I'd done it quite well. I was wearing my oldest jeans because they fit me the best, my new trainers because Mia and Chloe thought they were absolutely brill with their plastic strandy bits on the sides, and my white shirt – because it's loose and doesn't show that my boobs are still as flat as pancakes.

'You look lovely!' said Mum as I went into the sitting room and sat down where I could keep an eye on the window.

I felt pleased. We all three watched the telly, only I wasn't really watching because my mind was full of that photo again, and why it was so important that Mum didn't know anything about it.

Fancy Matt having a secret from Mum. Well, it was obvious he'd have secrets from her, because everyone has secrets from their mum – but I mean a big, important secret that made him come home specially to explain it to me so I wouldn't spill the beans. The more I thought about it, the more incredible it seemed.

I glanced at Mum. She'd said I looked

lovely, but I knew I'd never look as nice as her. She's older than my friends' mothers, but she doesn't look it. She's very slim with shoulder-length ash blonde hair and a really relaxed way of moving. It doesn't matter whether she's sitting or standing or walking or just unloading the washing machine, she always looks really good. She hasn't got a proper paid job, but she spends hours and hours helping out in one of the local primary schools. She's taken over as the librarian there, but she also hears children reading, and does anything else the head teacher wants her to do.

'That sounds like the old banger!' said Dad.

My eyes shot to the window. He was right. Matt's dirty yellow Citroën was pulling up outside.

'He's home!' I cried, jumping up and practically clapping my hands like a little girl.

Mum and Dad exchanged a bit of a *smug parents* look. They loved it that I was so fond of my big brother. Then we all rushed to get to the front door. I won.

'Hi, everybody! How'ya doing?' Matt said breezily as he strolled up the front path, his dirty limp little rucksack slung over his shoulder, his long hair tied back in a pony-tail. 'Nice welcome, but I think you forgot the red carpet, didn't you?'

I stood back so Mum could give her precious son a big hug.

Then Dad did the same. 'Travelling light as usual, Matt?'

He grinned. 'Well, not exactly . . . Hiya, Kates! Going on to a film set?' I didn't get him at first, then I realised he was talking about my make-up. I wished I hadn't bothered. I felt stupid now. 'Hang on a sec . . .'

He went back to the car and started heaving plastic bags out of the boot. 'Just a bit of washing, Mum. Nothing much.'

Mum was pretending to be appalled, but

of course she didn't mind in the slightest really. We took a bag each and dumped them in front of the washing machine. Then, as Mum loaded up the first wash and Dad put the kettle on, Matt talked about a film he'd been to see last night. It sounded quite good, but I was only half listening. The rest of me was wondering how much longer I'd have to wait until we'd be on our own and I could ask him the big question.

It turned out to be ten minutes.

'OK, I'll just go and check you haven't got a paid lodger in my room,' grinned Matt.

I followed him out and rushed after him as he leaped upstairs two at a time.

In his room he started fiddling with his old radio. (He'd taken his new CD player and radio and everything he needed to his flat at uni.) I sat on the bed and wondered whether he was going to tell me or whether I'd have to ask. He suddenly bobbed down, opened the bottom drawer of his desk, pulled out the photo and sat on the bed beside me. I didn't say a word.

'Look, Katie . . .' He didn't sound too happy. 'I really wish you hadn't gone rummaging through my things, you know.'

'But I was only looking for a battery. I didn't rummage. I just found it.'

'The thing is, it's got nothing to do with you. It's just that I don't want Mum to know about it.'

'Why not?'

'Because she'd be upset.'

'Would Dad?'

'Yes, but not so much.'

I waited. He was staring at the photo, his head bent over it.

'Yeah?'

'OK, I'll tell you who they are, these people, on condition that you promise that once I've told you – you won't *do* anything.' I swallowed.

I didn't have a clue what I could possibly want to do. He turned to look at me properly. 'Promise?'

I nodded.

'OK.'

I waited.

'You know our real dad?'

I gulped. 'M-Martin?'

'Well, he's got another son.'

Goose bumps were coming up all over my arms.

'A son? No, he hasn't! I once asked Mum if Martin and Dawn had got any children and she said they hadn't.' (It felt so weird saying the name of the stranger who was my father.)

'That's right. *They* haven't. I'm talking about a son he had with his *first* wife. You know he was married *before* he married Mum, don't you?'

I swallowed. I had known that, but it seemed so far away from me and my life that I hadn't been the slightest bit interested – until now.

'Did – did you know Martin's other son from when you were a little boy?'

'No, not really. I've got this vague recollection that he once came to our house, but I've always known about his existence.'

My heart was beating loudly. The kitchen was right below Matt's room. I could hear Mum singing as she moved about tidying up or whatever she was doing.

I lowered my voice to a whisper, even though there was no way she'd hear me. 'So . . . you've kept in touch with him?'

He didn't answer.

'Mum thinks you haven't seen Martin for years,' I went on.

'I haven't.'

A big feeling of relief swept through me. Mum wouldn't be hurt after all. Matt had been mistaken.

'I've only been in touch with him

occasionally – by phone. The last time was two or three years ago. And I never saw his son after Martin left Mum for Dawn.' I knew there was more to come. 'But ... then I tracked him down about eighteen months ago because I wanted to know what my half-brother was like.'

My eyes widened and I felt dizzy as something hit me. 'He's – he's *my* half-brother too, isn't he?'

Matt nodded and pointed to the woman in the photo. 'And that's his wife. It was taken about a year ago.'

'They're so young – for grown-ups!'

'Thirty-six.'

But I was staring at the picture of my half-brother. 'So that's him. It's really ... incredible.' My brain was trying to absorb all that Matt was telling me. 'And you know him.'

'Yeah, we're quite close now.'

I swallowed. Mum was still singing away

in the kitchen. I felt guilty about having this conversation.

Matt suddenly spoke quickly and urgently as though he'd read my mind. 'But Mum mustn't know. She'd be really upset if she knew. She hates Martin – I mean *hates* him – because of the way he used to drink, and I think he was quite cruel to her. She can't bear to think that you and I are anything to do with him.' Matt turned his head sharply to check how I was taking it all.

'But this is his son, not him.' I knew I was sounding naïve. 'His son doesn't drink a lot . . . or anything, does he?'

'No, of course not. He's not even in touch with his dad either – our dad. It's just the very fact that he *is* Martin's son, and like I said, Mum doesn't want us to have anything to do with Martin.' Matt's eyes were flashing. I could tell he really wanted me to get it. 'Not *anything*, Kates. So that includes hanging out with his son. I know I've never really said anything much to you about all this before – I might have done if you'd been the same age as me. But Martin was so horrible to her, you see . . .' Matt was biting his nails and frowning. I could tell he hated having this conversation with me. 'And then leaving her like that when you were only a baby – Mum's totally closed that chapter of her life.'

'But it's not –'

'– Chris's fault. No, I know. But take it from me, Mum would still be upset.'

Chris. So my half-brother was called Chris.

'Why? I still don't get *why* she'd be upset.'

'Look, it's not something anyone can explain. You just have to accept it. I once tested the waters with her. Really casually. I said, "It's funny to think I've got a half-brother that I've never even met, isn't it?"'

'Had you met him then?' I interrupted in a whisper.

He shook his head.

'What did she say?'

'She just looked a bit shaken and said, "Lots of people have got half-brothers and -sisters and stepbrothers and -sisters these days. It's the people you've grown up with that count." Then she looked me in the eyes and said, "It's painful for me to think about the past, Matt. It's best kept buried."'

I was shell-shocked, and sat there thinking about everything I'd just found out.

Matt must have thought I wasn't convinced. 'For God's sake, Katie, Mum even changed our surname from Marchant to Oriss so that she and Dad and you and I would all have the same surname and every last trace of our real dad would be wiped out. She wants everyone to think that Dad is our real dad.'

I was silent for a few seconds but my mind was racing away.

'What's his wife called?' I asked in a small

voice because I didn't know what else to say, but I was desperate to keep Matt talking. I knew my brother, and any second now the shutters would suddenly come down and he'd say, *Right, that's it. End of conversation.*

'She's called Claire. And their daughter is Laura.'

I drew the photo closer to have another good look at Laura. But it dropped into my lap because my fingers were trembling so much. I'd suddenly realised why Laura looked familiar. I knew exactly who she reminded me of now.

Me.

3 SHARING THE SECRET

Next morning I woke up with a start. I'd been dreaming that I had a twin and she was stuck inside a mountain living with a bunch of cave-men who didn't understand that she wasn't one of them. My eyes flew open and I shot up. *Laura! My twin was Laura!*

Then my mobile beeped to tell me I'd got a text. I blinked a few times to get rid of the dream, and read the message. It was from Chloe. She wanted to know if I could meet her and Mia and another friend of ours, Emily, at Streeters asap. I texted back *OK. Seeya* because

I couldn't be bothered to write any more. It was like I needed every single bit of my mind to focus on Matt's news. I really wanted to talk to him again and find out more. *And* have another look at the photo.

I crept into his room. He was fast asleep, just a hump under the duvet. It wouldn't matter, would it? I tiptoed over to his desk and opened the bottom drawer as quietly as possible. The photo wasn't there. It must be hidden. I pulled the drawer right out and looked through everything. But it definitely wasn't there. I glanced over to the bed. The hump hadn't moved.

One by one I tried all the drawers. No photo. So then I went over to the bedside chair. It must be in one of his pockets. As I gently lifted up his jeans, loads of coins fell out of one of the back pockets and rattled on the floorboards between the rugs.

Matt's head appeared like a tortoise

emerging from its shell. He was squinting in the light and his hair was sticking out all over the place. 'What are you doing?' he said gruffly.

I bent down to pick up the coins and hide my guilty-looking face.

'As if I couldn't guess,' he added, rubbing his eyes. 'Just leave it alone, Katie! It's nothing to do with you. Forget it, OK?'

I saw the photo sticking out of his other back pocket so I sat down and looked at it, but he snatched it off me and stuffed it under his pillow.

'Matt!'

'Are you listening to me, Katie? *It's nothing to do with you. Get it?*'

'But I can't stop thinking about it. It *is* something to do with me. I even dreamt about Laura.'

He closed his eyes and opened them again slowly, as though he was despairing of me.

'She's just a girl.'

'Does she know about me?'

'I dunno.'

'You must know.'

'I might have mentioned you. But she's got her own life.'

'How old is she?'

'I dunno. Thirteen.'

'Is she nice?'

'Yeah, just ordinary.' He folded his arms. 'Look, can you go away and stop pestering me? I don't know them *that* well or anything . . .'

'Have you told Jen about them?'

'Course I have. Anyway, she's coming down today. She's got some tops or something for you.'

'Oh, brilliant!'

Jen is Matt's girlfriend. They started going out with each other right at the beginning of their first year at university and moved into a flat together at the beginning of their second year. She's really lovely and so generous. Just about every time I see her these days she gives me some sort of present – like perfume or moisturiser or an old bag or a belt that she doesn't use any more. But some tops! That sounded great.

'What time's she coming?'

'Lunchtime. Ish.'

Even better. I'd go and meet Chloe and the others, then come back and see Jen.

They were sitting at the table in the corner of Streeters, with big frothy milkshakes in front of them.

'You've got to get strawberry, Kate!' called Chloe the moment I walked through the door. 'We're sharing.'

I knew what she meant. We often did this. We each order a different flavour and drink exactly half, then pass them round, pouring in bits from each other's to make a really weird flavour and an even weirder colour. Matt thought it sounded disgusting when I told him, but we like doing it.

'So did you have fun last night?' I asked them when I'd ordered the milkshake and sat down.

'We all fell asleep in front of the video,' giggled Emily.

'It wasn't much good,' Chloe said. 'The video, I mean.'

'Really boring,' added Mia, rolling her eyes.

'We woke up at seven,' went on Chloe, 'but I didn't think you'd appreciate being texted so early.'

I smiled vaguely and wondered how I was going to wangle it so I could be on my own with Chloe for long enough to tell her the secret. I'd spent ages last night lying in bed wondering whether the thing about not telling anyone still applied now, or whether it was only really Mum and Dad I shouldn't tell. The trouble was, I'd feel totally mean and horrible if my friends all knew my brother's big secret and my mum didn't. So I'd come up with the compromise of telling just Chloe and swearing her to secrecy.

'We're going to look round the shops after this,' said Emily. 'Are you coming?'

I nodded. Good plan. I'd be able to fix it so I was on my own with Chloe, then I could tell her. 'I've got to be back by twelve-thirty. Jen's coming.'

Chloe looked at her watch. 'Omigod! *I* was supposed to be back five minutes ago. Mum said I could come out with you lot on condition I got her some coriander, and made sure I was back by eleven. She's got loads of people coming for dinner.'

I felt myself panicking, then I told myself to calm down. This was ridiculous. It simply meant I had to put off telling Chloe my news for a while. So what was the big deal?

'Just going to the loo,' she said, getting up.

The urgency came back. 'Me too.' I was praying that the others wouldn't suddenly decide they wanted to go too.

'Chloe,' I hissed the moment we got downstairs. 'Something amazing's happened . . .'

She stopped in her tracks. 'What? What?' She was gripping my hand. Chloe's always been like that – touchy. I mean the nice sort of touchy.

I knew I'd have to gabble to say as much as I wanted to say before we had to get back to the others. 'I found this photo in Matt's room. I couldn't tell you because he made me promise not to tell anyone. It was during the week. And I texted him and he phoned me and said whatever I did I mustn't show Mum or Dad.'

Chloe gasped and gripped my other hand as well. 'What was it? Something really . . . rude?'

'No, nothing like that. It turns out that Matt and I have got a half-brother and Matt's actually tracked him down!'

'Half-brother? What half-brother? I've never heard you mention any half-brothers.'

'I didn't know he even existed! That's why it's so incredible. Only Mum doesn't know Matt's met him because it would upset her too much.'

'Omigod, Kates! A half-brother! That's so cool! What's he like? Is he good looking? How old is he? Can I go out with him?'

Chloe was gripping my elbows now.

'No, of course not. He's far too –'

'– too young. Yeah, course! Silly me. He must be younger than you, because your real dad didn't meet that other woman till after you were born, did he?' She stopped talking and her eyes opened really wide. 'Oh. Right. I get it. Your real father's just had a baby! Wow, he's quite old for a father, isn't he? Is that why it's such a big thing? Is it going to be in the papers or something?'

'No, no. Ssh, Chlo! Listen! My half-brother's not a baby. He's older than me – older than Matt. Much older. He's my real father's son by his first marriage – before he met Mum even. He's a grown man with a daughter of thirteen. She's called Laura. But Mum's got no idea that Matt's met them all and he's getting to know them and everything.'

Chloe stopped gripping my elbows, thank goodness. But it was only because she couldn't hang on for a second longer. Her hands dropped to her sides, like the shock had weakened all her muscles.

She spoke slowly, in a breathy whisper, as though she'd just worked out a really difficult problem. 'So you're . . .'

'I'm what?'

'You're Laura's . . . aunt!'

Then it was *my* turn to gasp. I'd never

thought of that. It was so weird. I was the same age as her, yet I was her aunt. And Matt wanted me to forget about it all.

How could I?

4 PLAYING WITH FIRE

I knew Jen had arrived the moment I went in the house. Her perfume smells so beautiful.

'Hiya!' I called out, and she came galloping downstairs.

'Hi, precious,' she said. She calls everyone over-the-top names – Honey, Precious, Sweetie. Matt says it's because she's a luvvie. He means she's a drama student. 'You look stunning!' She held me at arm's length and made a big thing of looking me up and down. 'More gorgeous every time I see you!' Then she kissed the air on either side of my cheeks, saying 'Mwah! Mwah!' as she did it.

I couldn't help smiling. That's the effect Jen has on everyone. I've no idea what she's doing with a dosser like my brother, as I keep telling her. She grabbed my hand and led me upstairs. 'Got some prezzies for you, darl! Come and see!'

The two tops were on Matt's bed. So was Matt, but the tops were more interesting. One was black and white and tight, and the other was pink with a hole (deliberate) just under one shoulder. 'They look brand new, Jen!'

'I know, but they don't suit me, and that's that. In fact I look hideous in them, whereas *you'll* look fantab!'

I took them to my room and tried them on. They were the nicest tops I'd ever worn. I'm not sure that I looked fantab exactly, but I was really pleased with them.

'Hi,' I said to the mirror. 'I'm Katie.'

'Hi, I'm Laura,' came the answer from inside my head.

I smiled at my niece and she smiled back. Then I clicked back to the here and now, because Jen had come in and I didn't want her to think I was really up myself.

'Perfect!' she said. Good, she hadn't noticed my one-to-one with the mirror. 'Utterly perfect!'

'Did they cost a lot?' I asked hesitantly.

'No – got them in a sale,' she said. 'I don't want anything for them. I'm just glad they're going to a good home.'

I went back into Matt's room with her because I wanted to talk about Laura, and I thought I might get a bit further now Jen was here. If Matt tried to shut me up, she'd be sure to tell him not to be so mean.

'Did Matt mention that I saw the photo of Chris and Claire and Laura?' I began.

'What? Oh . . . yeah. I think so.' She was trying to sound all vague, but her eyes flashed a kind of warning, so then I knew that she and

Matt must have been talking about me. It suddenly bugged me. How come it was OK for Jen to know about my half-brother and my niece when *I* wasn't supposed to? Her lips were pursed as though she disapproved. This wasn't like Jen. Why had she changed so quickly? One minute she was all friendly and giving me new tops, then the next . . . Wait a minute – maybe that's what the two new tops were about. I could just imagine Matt and her talking . . .

For God's sake, get down here and take Katie's mind off Chris.
How am I going to do that?
I dunno. Bring her some clothes or something.
Yeah, OK. I've got these two tops . . .
Wicked.

I felt cross and left out, but I tried to hide it by sounding mature and matter-of-fact. 'Tell me how you found out where they lived,' I asked Matt. 'Was it from Martin?'

'Nope.'

I waited.

He spoke in a tired voice. 'It happened by mistake, OK?'

Then he heaved a big sigh and fell silent as though the story was too long and complicated and he didn't have the energy to carry on.

Jen glanced at him then took up the story herself. It wasn't her usual style of talking, though. This was a Jen I didn't recognise – a kind of subdued, hesitant version of the real thing. 'Matt knew from Martin that . . . Chris had done chemistry at university and that he'd gone on to work in some big research company. And that made Matt feel a kind of link with Chris – you can imagine, them both being into chemistry.' She glanced at me and I nodded quickly. 'But Martin and Chris are hardly in touch with each other any more, so that was a bit of a dead end.'

'Yeah,' said Matt, getting into it a bit more now that Jen had got him started, 'and I was just reading this science magazine one day, because it had an article on the very subject I needed for one of my modules, when I got a shock because it said *Chris Marchant* at the end. And I realised I'd just read something that might well have been written by my own half-brother.'

I wanted to speak, but I made myself stay quiet as a shadow because Matt was staring at the wall in a sort of trance. It was like he was reliving the whole thing and had completely forgotten he was at home in his own room, with a sister who wouldn't stop pestering him. 'So I got talking to one of the professors and I casually mentioned that I'd read this article by Chris Marchant, and he told me that Chris was giving a talk in a couple of weeks' time in Reading, so I decided to go.'

'Did you tell your lecturer that Chris was your half-brother?'

'No. Course not. I wasn't going to broadcast that. You never know how things are going to spread. I didn't want there to be any chance of Mum finding out.'

Matt was starting to get wound up, so Jen tried to calm things down. 'His lecturer didn't think there was anything odd about a chemistry student going to a talk by a well-known chemist.'

'And anyway, there was no reason to make any connection between me and Chris,' Matt added. 'I'm Matt Oriss, he's Chris Marchant.'

'And you weren't even sure that this was the right Chris Marchant, were you?'

'Exactly.'

They had me gripped. This was real-life drama. 'So what happened then?'

'Well, I went . . . and I thought I saw a bit of a resemblance to Martin, but I wasn't certain.' Matt was getting restless, rubbing his neck. I could tell he felt uncomfortable about telling me the next bit. I prompted him gently. 'Yeah? So did you talk to him at the end?'

'Uh-huh.' There was a long pause while Matt stared straight ahead of him, then he suddenly snapped out of his trance and spoke abruptly. 'And that's it, really. It *was* him. So there you go.'

I couldn't believe this . . . I was bursting with excitement because we'd got to the most important bit, and here was Matt skating over it like it was nothing. 'But what did you say? What did *he* say? Was it really incredible?'

Matt sighed, then went back into his trance as quickly as he'd come out of it. 'I can't remember what I said. I'd got something all planned, but when it came to it, whatever I said was entirely different. We exchanged phone numbers and that was it.'

I'd been holding my breath, but I let it

out, disappointed. The drama seemed to be fizzling away.

'What do you mean, that was it? Did you phone him? Where was he living? Was it near your university?'

'Yeah, only about twenty minutes away. I didn't phone him though because I felt guilty, going behind Mum's back. Jen said I should leave it a couple of days and see how I felt then. So I did. But on the second day *he* phoned *me* and invited me round to his house. It was completely different after that, because he seemed like a real person once I'd met him properly with his family.' Matt got up and started looking through the pile of ironing that Mum had left on the bed. He was giving me the signal that the conversation really was over this time. That was OK. I didn't need to talk. I'd got enough to think about. I stood there like a cardboard cut-out, going through it all in my head.

A wife, a daughter, real people. I was picturing Matt in the midst of this brand-new family, laughing and having fun. I sat down on his bed and hugged my knees. 'I bet Laura thought it was wicked finding out that she'd got a new kind of uncle, didn't she?'

Matt shrugged, but he was looking pretty pleased with himself and I could imagine Laura thought he was great.

'So do you and Chris . . .' I didn't know how to say what I meant . . . '*feel* like brothers?'

Matt shrugged again. 'Yeah, I suppose,' he said.

'You *suppose*!' laughed Jen. She suddenly sprang to life. 'That's a bit of an understatement! You two have got all the important things in common. Chris is a total honey – wicked sense of humour, laid-back big time, utterly wrapped up in boring chemical things, generous and kind . . . and always so pleased to see us.'

I gasped. So this was what had been going on behind my back.

Matt groaned softly and Jen went red. She realised she'd made a big mistake, but it was too late.

'Sounds like you both know him pretty well,' I said, trying desperately not to sound like a little girl in a big stress, but failing.

Jen looked down. That said it all.

I flew at Matt. 'So your girlfriend's allowed to meet our family, but your sister isn't! Great!'

Matt jumped up and spoke in his most urgent voice while Jen stood at his side, her hands clenched. 'But you were only a baby when Martin left. I was six. I had some history with him. There's no reason for you to open up that closed chapter. Think about Mum. It'd destroy her.'

'Then I'll have to do what *you* did, and do it behind her back.'

But even as I was saying it, I wasn't sure that I'd be able to go ahead.

Jen shot Matt a *How are you going to deal with that?* look.

Matt just put his head in his hands, so Jen took over. She was trying to be reasonable. It didn't suit her. 'Come on, Kates, you don't want to upset your mum, do you? And if you meet Chris and you two really hit it off, what happens then?'

For the first time ever I felt like telling Jen to butt out and mind her own business. 'What's it got to do with you?'

I stomped out of the room and ran downstairs, but before I got to the bottom, Matt had caught up with me. He grabbed my arm and spoke shakily, his eyes darting towards the kitchen door. 'OK, calm down! We'll sort it out.'

'When?'

'Next weekend.' He leaned over the banister

towards the kitchen. We both knew Mum was in there, cooking. 'Ssh!' he said, putting a finger to his lips.

I looked at him through narrow eyes. 'Promise, next weekend?'

'Promise.'

But that wasn't enough. I had to be sure. I stuck my hand out. He sighed and shook it. 'You're playing with fire,' he whispered.

'*You* started it.'

'Matt and Jen have invited me up to their place next weekend,' I announced brightly, my heart hammering.

We were sitting round the table later, eating curry – my favourite. The telly was on in the background and people's eyes kept drifting to and from the screen – except for Matt's, which stayed glued to it.

'Oh!' said Mum.

Out of the corner of my eye I could see her

puzzled face. She was probably wondering what on earth there would be for a fourteen-year-old to do all weekend with her student brother and his girlfriend. But Mum wouldn't just come out and say that, though, in case Matt thought she was putting a damper on the idea.

'Katie's never seen round the whole campus,' beamed Jen. She made it sound like I was getting a guided tour of Buckingham Palace.

'Ooh! Lovely,' Mum sounded a bit more enthusiastic.

'Where will she sleep?' Dad asked Matt.

'On the sofa,' said Matt, his eyes scarcely leaving the screen.

'Is that OK, Mum?' I thought I'd better ask.

'Well, I don't see why not,' she said. 'As long as Matt and Jen are happy, it's fine with us, isn't it, Richard?'

'Absolutely,' Dad said, putting his hands up as though it was nothing to do with him.

Sometimes I wish my parents weren't so nice. It would make things like deceiving them much easier. My cheeks were beginning to burn – and not because of the curry.

5 BREAKING THE ICE

The following Saturday morning at eight-thirty I gave Mum and Dad a big hug each and got on to the train.

'See you tonight! 'Byeee!'

My head felt crammed to the brim with emotions as I flopped back in my seat and the train chugged out of the station. In the end Matt had decided it would be best if I just went for the day. But what an exciting day it was going to be. So why did I feel so guilty?

As the train gathered speed Jen's million-pound question came into my head: *And if you meet Chris and you two really hit it off, what happens then?* She'd asked me the same question twice on the phone during the week.

'That won't happen,' I'd told her, quite aggressively. But we both knew I was only cross because I couldn't come up with an answer. I was stopping myself from thinking beyond today.

I stared out of the window, and the world outside fast-forwarded while I sat there with my thoughts. There was Mum, Dad, Matt, Jen and Chloe. Those were the people I 'hit it off with', as Jen puts it. I'd known Chloe since playgroup, so she was practically one of the family. I couldn't imagine being that close to anyone else. I mean, Chris is a grown man in his thirties. He isn't going to feel anything like a brother, is he? It would probably be more the kind of relationship I've got with my older cousins – Dad's sister's children. I don't hit it off with *them*. I see them about three times a year. We all sit round talking, knowing we've got nothing in common. I expect they're always dying for it to be time for us lot to go. *I* certainly am. Then we can heave a big sigh of relief until the next time.

By the time the train pulled in at the station I felt exhausted from thinking round and round the same subject for nearly an hour. Well, more like a week, actually.

We started the university tour with the theatre where Jen spent so much of her time.

'Welcome to Theatre Land!' she said dramatically as we crept in through the back door. We walked down a little passage and came out by the wings. There wasn't a soul about, so I took centre stage and pretended to be the compere at a Royal Variety Performance. That lasted about ten seconds, because I'm quite self-conscious really. Jen took over and made us crack up with her over-the-top gestures.

After that she gave us a tour of the whole theatre, so I got to see the lighting and sound areas, the little dressing rooms and everything.

Next we went to look at Matt's lab. 'And this is *my* territory,' he said, unlocking the door and flinging it open.

I stared round the gleaming white clinical-looking room. 'It's no good, I can't imagine you in a white coat, looking down a microscope, Matt.'

'Cheers.'

'I'll have you know he looks fantab in white!' said Jen, winking at me.

I glanced at her in her cut-off jeans and stripy little top, and wondered for the hundredth time why a stylish person like her got on so well with a rather weird, scruffy chemist like Matt. Then I forgot all about that because my stomach suddenly did an amazing backflip. I was going to meet my half-brother. It was nearly time.

Something must have shown on my face. 'Getting excited, Katie?'

No, I mustn't let myself get excited. It's no big deal. It'll be no different from meeting those boring cousins.

'A bit.'

We left the university campus and went into town to look round a few shops. At lunchtime we shared a massive pizza, then we got into the car and set off. I knew the journey to Chris's place was going to take about twenty-five minutes, so there was plenty of time to settle back and watch the world go by again. But I couldn't. I sat bolt upright the whole way, my heart beating more and more quickly the nearer we got.

'OK, this is it,' said Matt, glancing at me through the driving mirror as we turned into a long straight road where all the houses looked identical.

I shot up even straighter in my seat.

'Don't look so worried,' smiled Jen, turning right round. 'Nobody's going to feed you to the sharks or make you drink arsenic, you know.'

Did I look that *scared?*

And then Matt pulled in behind a white Ford and we all piled out.

I walked up the front path behind Matt and Jen, in such a daze that I didn't realise that the door to the house had already opened. When I looked up I saw a pretty woman with short, dark brown hair standing in the doorway. She looked exactly as she did in the photo. So this was Chris's wife.

'Hi,' she said, rushing out to give Matt and Jen big hugs and kisses. 'It's so lovely to see you all.' She gave me a quick hug and said, 'Hi, Katie. I'm Claire. It's great to meet you.'

I was too nervous to speak, so I just smiled, feeling suddenly childish. She ushered us all into the hall and I noticed how dark it seemed compared with the bright light outside. 'Come through – I think they're both in the garden.' She turned to smile at me. I obviously looked cold. 'Let's tell them to come in. It's freezing, isn't it?'

'Love your earrings, Claire,' said Jen.

'Thanks,' smiled Claire. 'Laura gave them to me last Mother's Day.'

Laura. Real live Laura. Her daughter, my niece . . . And I was just about to meet her.

We'd reached the back door. It was open. Matt and Jen were blocking my view. I followed them outside.

'This is Chris,' said Matt to me.

And suddenly there he was – my half-brother. I didn't know what to do or say. He was smiling his way up to me, ready to shake hands. My hand felt like a little crumpled hanky in his strong grip.

'Hello, Katie. It's great that you could come. Laura's been so excited – well, I mean, we've all been excited . . .'

I was still struck dumb. *Why? I'm not usually like this. Pull yourself together, Katie.* He was good looking, my brother was. He'd got a beard, which he didn't have in the photo, quite long hair and a really nice smile. His brown eyes were twinkling at me, and all I could think was, *You're nothing like those cousins of mine!*

'Hi.'

I turned round and there was Laura. The first thing I noticed was her shoulders. She'd hunched them up like a little girl – all worried. Her hair was in a ponytail with a few bits hanging down at the front, just like mine. It was the same colour as mine too – kind of mousy. She broke into a smile and I said, 'Hi.' Then we didn't know what to say next. She went and stood by her mum, and her mum put her arm round her. I wished my mum was here to put her arm round me . . .

And then it hit me. Mum had no idea that

I was here, meeting Martin's son. She'd trusted me and I'd gone behind her back. At that very moment my phone bleeped softly. Laura heard it too and our eyes met as I pulled it out of my bag.

'You're so lucky, having a mobile,' she said. 'Is it one of your friends?'

'I looked at the text message. *Saw poetry book you need. Bought it! Love Mum XX.*

'No . . . it's my mum.'

The grown-ups had all stopped talking and were looking at me.

'Everything all right?' Matt asked me anxiously.

I nodded and tried to smile. But it wasn't all right. It was all wrong.

I shouldn't be here. It's a big mistake. Poor, poor Mum.

'I've made a cake,' said Claire, taking her arm away from Laura's shoulder and putting it round mine. I thought I might throw up if I tried to eat any cake. I shivered. 'Come on, let's go inside,' she went on brightly.

Jen rushed up to the back door, making everyone laugh. 'Good, I'm glad you said that, sweetie, because I've got the most terrible circulation, and I would hate my fingers to drop off all over your garden.'

I looked at Laura. She was smiling at what Jen had just said. Our eyes met and the smile turned into one for each other.

'I want to hear all about what you've been getting up to,' said Chris as we went into the sitting room. 'Come and sit by me.'

So I did, but I didn't know what to say. 'Um . . .'

'Start by telling me about your school.'

'Dad!' said Laura, sounding a bit embarrassed. 'Katie doesn't want to talk about her school.'

'OK, it doesn't have to be school,' said Chris. 'How about friends?'

'Erm . . . Well, there's Chloe – she's my best friend – and then –'

'Hey, my best friend's called Chloe too!' said Laura, sitting on the floor. 'Well, she's quite a good friend, anyway. What does *your* Chloe look like?'

So I described mine, and Laura described hers, and they were completely different, but as we'd discovered they had the same name, we both wanted them to have everything the same, so we started twisting things to make them seem more similar.

'My Chloe absolutely loves chocolate,' said Laura.

I thought about my Chloe. She wasn't into chocolate. She preferred bitter fruity sweets. 'And mine loves chocolate milkshake!' I said.

'Hey, that's incredible!' said Laura. 'Guess what, Dad?' But Chris was discussing car engines with Matt by then, and didn't hear her. So Laura turned to Claire. 'Hey, guess what, Mum?'

Claire and Jen were deep in conversation about face massages.

'It was just the *moooooost* relaxing thing ever, hon,' Jen was saying, her eyes closed and her head tilted backwards, as though she was having a face massage right that very minute. She looked so funny, I couldn't help a little snigger escaping. That made Laura giggle too. Her mum shot her a bit of a mummish look and Laura clapped her hand over her mouth, but I could tell she was still giggling underneath, because her eyes were all crinkled up and nearly watering. That set *me* off too, and in the end Laura squashed on to the settee beside me and whispered, 'Shall we go up to my room?'

I nodded and we got up awkwardly, then crept out to the sound of Jen describing the candles that were burning during her massage.

The moment we were out of the room I couldn't help it, I just broke into a big giggling fit and so did Laura. We could hardly climb the stairs we were laughing so much.

'Ssh! They'll hear us,' said Laura, her eyes still watering.

'But the scent was positively alluring, sweetie!' I replied.

And that made Laura even worse.

We somehow staggered into her room and then I stopped laughing because there was so much to look at.

On the wall above her bed was a theatre mask. 'Oh, wow! Matt gave one of those to Jen for her birthday.'

'Dad gave me this one,' said Laura.

I nodded. 'Do you like acting?'

She giggled. 'Yeah, but I'm not very good at it.'

'I'm hopeless.'

'Do you like horses?'

I shook my head. 'Not really.'

'Me neither.'

'What about cooking?'

'Yeah . . .'

'Me too.'

She dragged me over to the window and pointed to two hutches at the far end of the garden. 'Do you like baby rabbits?'

'Yeah! Cool!'

'They're only a week old.'

'Oh, sweet! Can I look?'

We rushed downstairs and on our way through the hall I heard Chris say, 'Well, the girls seem to be getting on OK.'

Matt didn't reply – unless I just didn't hear him.

6 HATE AND DECEIT

'So how did you get on?' said Mum.

It was eight-thirty that evening. We'd met on the platform. She was all smiles but I was a bag of nerves.

'It was . . . really good.'

'Did you get my text message about the poetry book, by the way?'

Thank goodness we could start with something easy. I'd been dreading launching into the lies.

'Yes, I got it.'

'I knew Matt was going to buy it for you if

you came across any bookshops, and I didn't want you to finish up with two copies.'

'We didn't actually see any.'

'Didn't you go into the town?'

'Yes . . . We had a pizza for lunch. It was a really lovely café.'

She was smiling away as she listened. And then we'd reached the car. *It'd be easier in the car with Mum staring straight ahead.*

'So what do you think of the flat? I bet it's a mess, isn't it?'

'Erm . . . we didn't go to their flat. Just looked round the university and the town.'

Mum seemed a bit surprised. 'Oh. Right. What did you think of the theatre?'

At least I was on safe ground here. 'It was really cool. They've got tons of scenery and lighting. There's even a rotating bit in the stage . . .' I knew I was gabbling. 'And I saw the lab where Matt works.'

She laughed. 'I bet that was interesting.'

'I just can't imagine Matt ever actually doing any work.'

'Well, let's hope he does! What did you do after you'd looked round the university?'

Here we go – the first lie.

'That's when we went for the pizza. Then we just looked round a bit – you know.'

There was a pause. Mum seemed to be concentrating on her driving. I was racking my brains for something else to say that wasn't a lie.

She spoke first. 'And what are Matt and Jen doing tonight?'

They're going out to dinner with Matt's brother and his wife.

'I think they're going out to dinner somewhere.'

'Ooh! Dinner!' Mum laughed. 'I didn't know Matt did grown-up things like that. I wonder whose influence that is?'

His brother's.

'What are we doing tomorrow, Mum?'

'Nothing planned.'

'Can I go round to Chloe's?'

'I don't see why not, love.'

'It was awful telling Mum all those lies, Chlo. Well, they weren't exactly lies, but I wasn't being honest and I hated it.'

Chloe and I were walking into town. I'd told her every single detail of what had happened at Chris's. She thought it sounded brilliant. 'Sometimes you have to tell your parents lies, don't you? I mean, we all do it.' She was trying to make me feel better. 'Like saying that videos are twelves when they're fifteens, and saying you did fine in a test when you actually got fourteen per cent.'

'But this is nothing like that. It's a whole big deceit. And it makes it worse because it's me *and* Matt.'

'I don't think you should feel bad, Kate. I mean, it's not like you're always seeing Chris and the others. You've only met them once, haven't you?'

I looked down. There was a short silence.

'Oh. Right,' she said, breathing out slowly. 'So you're planning on getting to know them . . . properly, are you?'

'I know I shouldn't, but I really like them. And he *is* my brother.'

'Well then, you've got to tell your mum. Couldn't you pretend you met them by chance yesterday, and they seemed very nice, so you don't see why you shouldn't be friends with them?'

Chloe really didn't get it. 'You're joking!' I squeaked. 'Met them by chance? How could that have happened? The only way we could possibly have met is on purpose.'

'I meant *you* met them by chance. Surely she won't mind that Matt has tracked them down, will she?'

I'd been so sure that Chloe had understood

the situation, but she hadn't, and that made me realise what a big thing I was getting myself into here.

'Matt's been keeping it a secret all this time because he knows how much it would mess Mum up, Chlo.'

I still wasn't sure if she understood. She was walking along frowning. But then she suddenly stopped and looked me straight in the eye. 'Well, if you're not going to tell, you've got two choices, Kate: *either* you stop seeing them *or* you carry on. If you carry on, then you'll have to keep it a secret from your mum and dad for ever.'

I gulped. She'd made it sound worse than it really was now. 'For ever?'

'Yeah. Imagine telling them in five years time that you've been living a lie for the last five years. They'd be doubly hurt, wouldn't they? One, because you've been seeing your half-brother and his family, and two, because you've been keeping it a secret for all that time.'

She was right. I let my breath out slowly. 'Oh Chlo, I don't know what to do.'

'What does Chris say?'

'He says it's been great to meet me and he'd love to keep in touch, but he doesn't want to upset anything, and it's up to me.'

'What about Laura?'

'I don't think it's ever crossed Laura's mind that we won't stay friends now we've met.'

'I've got a good idea, Kate.'

'I'm glad someone has.'

'Why not do nothing at all and see what happens?'

She was looking at me, all bright-eyed, as though she'd just given me her best dress which I'd been wanting for ages.

So I didn't do anything. *Great advice, Chlo.* That evening I got an e-mail from Laura. She'd written it yesterday.

Hi Katie,

It was so cool meeting up at last, wasn't it? I'd been dying to meet you because I wanted to see what my aunt looked like! Mum doesn't have any brothers or sisters and Dad's only got Matt, so you and Matt are my only aunt and uncle! Mum and Dad really like you, by the way. They think you and I have got a lot in common. This afternoon when you were here, I kept on trying to get the courage to say something to you about your mum hating my grandfather and all that. But I didn't dare in case it kind of put you off me. All I wanted to say was that it's nothing to do with us, is it? We can still be friends, can't we?

Anyway I'd better go. Write back if you can.

Lots of love, Laura XX

Why was Laura talking about *my* mum hating

her grandfather? I didn't get it. But then I realised that of course Laura's grandfather is my actual dad! What a horrible thought. I shut my eyes to make it go away. But it wouldn't, because it wasn't just a thought. You can make thoughts go away, but you can't make facts go away. I wanted to reply to Laura, but I didn't want to talk about mothers and grandfathers and hate and stuff.

I got as far as *Dear Laura*, then I couldn't think of anything to write, so in the end I deleted the *Dear Laura* and went downstairs.

Mum and Dad were watching a film. They were deep into it. I wished they weren't, because I urgently felt like talking. Although I was totally scared to go anywhere near the subject, I badly wanted a reaction from Mum. It might help me to know what to do.

'What time does this finish?' I asked quietly.

'Soon.'

I couldn't wait.

I started gabbling. 'Matt said that he thinks Martin's son did chemistry at university too.'

There, I'd said it. My heart was beating at about three hundred miles per hour.

'How does Matt know that?' Mum said, the words coming out of her mouth like bullets. Her eyes were boring into me.

Dad had taken hold of her hand, as if to calm her down.

I tried to sound casual, even though I could hardly breathe. 'Dunno. I suppose Martin must have told him ages ago, or something.'

'Mmm.'

Her eyes shot back to the screen, but they were flashing dangerously and I could tell she was still thinking about what I'd just said.

It took all the courage in the world to keep going. And I had to be very careful. 'I know you hate Martin because he left us, but do you hate his son too?'

Mum closed her eyes slowly and opened them again. 'I don't want anyone or anything that has *anything* to do with that man ever to enter my life, Katie. You can't be expected to understand that, because you're not old enough, and you were only a baby when he left. It's not that I have any personal hate for his son, just that I –'

Her voice cracked and Dad stepped in. 'Your mum went through a terrible time, love. It's best to leave it alone. There's nothing to be gained by digging it up.'

I stared at the carpet and wished I'd never spoken.

7 COMPLICATIONS

The next day after school the phone rang. Mum answered and I knew straight away that it was Matt. Her face turned all soft and smiley, and she sat down as though she was ready for a nice long chat. On the kitchen table in front of her was a pile of holiday brochures. She'd said we'd look at them together as soon as she'd made tea.

Listening to Mum's side of the phone conversation, I started to imagine what our family must seem like to other people. It was such gooey talk, all peppered with 'darlings' and sympathetic, motherly noises. I looked at the brochures and thought about our annual holidays. For the last few years I've been allowed to take a friend. It's always been Chloe. She loves coming on holiday with us. 'Your parents are so lovely and generous,' she always says. But I can't help questioning everything now, and I'm wondering if what she really means is, *You're so spoilt, aren't you?*

I expect I am a bit spoilt, but what can I do about it? I can hardly say, *No, don't take me on holiday to lovely places, and don't let me take a friend, and definitely don't let me do any jet-skiing when we're there, whatever you do!*

'Matt wants to speak to you, darling,' said Mum, handing me the phone.

'Hiya, Kates,' he said straight away. 'You might want to take it in your room or something. Be subtle though, yeah?'

I couldn't think of a single subtle way of leaving the kitchen, so I just walked out.

'What?' I asked as I climbed the stairs.

'It's Laura's birthday next Saturday. It was all arranged that she was going ten-pin bowling with her mum, her dad, me, Jen and three of her mates. Now it seems one of her mates can't come, and Laura is begging and begging for you to come.'

I didn't have to think at all. I was so happy. 'Oh, wicked!' I breathed. 'I'd really love to. I can't wait!'

'I kind of thought that's what you might say,' said Matt, sighing. 'Now we've got to work out what to tell Mum and Dad.'

I lay on my bed, my mouth going a bit dry, and dropped my voice to a whisper, just in case. 'Let's say it's something to do with Jen.'

'Yeah, I already decided that was our only option, because she'd think it was a bit odd if I invited you up to uni for the second weekend on the trot. Tell her Jen's in a play. Pretend we were talking about it last weekend, and Jen had the part of understudy to the main, only now it turns out that the girl in the main part's fallen ill so Jen's taking over.'

'It sounds a bit complicated.'

'You're right, Katie. It *is* complicated. What did you have to find that photo for?'

That was unfair of him. 'Why did you have to leave it where I could find it?'

His voice turned really snappy. 'This phone call's costing me a fortune. Let's wind it up. Go and ask Mum if you can come. It's a matinee, remember.'

I suddenly didn't want to. I couldn't face the lie. 'Can *you* ask her, Matt?'

He sighed a massive sigh. 'Get her to ring me back then.'

And with that he rang off.

'Whoa! Strike! I am *too too* exceptionally fab at this!'

Everyone laughed at Jen's big jubilation. Even one or two people in the lanes on either side were grinning over at her.

Matt looked embarrassed. 'She's a drama student!' he explained, with an apologetic look on his face.

'Be quiet!' said Jen. 'I can't help being a bit extrovert.'

'Mad, more like!' I told her.

And everyone laughed.

'Your go, Kates,' said Chris.

It was nice the way he'd started calling me Kates like Matt does.

'Go for it, Katie,' said Laura, picking out the purple ball that she knew I liked best.

We were playing in pairs. Guess who was *my* partner?

I bowled it as hard as I could, but it only knocked down three skittles.

'Doesn't matter,' Laura whispered, linking her arm through mine.

'Sorry you've got such a rubbish partner, Laura.'

'You're not rubbish.'

'We can swap round for the next game. Matt won't mind putting up with me. He's used to me.'

'No, I want us to stay together.'

And that's exactly what we did. Right to the end of her birthday treat. As it happened I got better as the game went on, so we came out second. Chris and Jen won.

Laura's other two friends, Ayesha and Sam, were really nice. They didn't seem at all jealous that Laura was so friendly with me. We all sat round a table drinking Coke and eating burgers and chips.

'It's so weird that you're Laura's auntie!' grinned Sam.

Ayesha looked puzzled. 'How come you have to keep it a secret from your mum?'

'It's difficult to explain . . .' I began.

Laura helped me out. 'Her mum'd be upset. My grandfather was horrible to her, you see.'

Ayesha was still frowning. 'Yeah, but –'

'Let's ask Mum if we can have puddings,' Laura interrupted her.

Ayesha didn't say any more. She'd got the message.

On the train I felt tense and guilty. I couldn't stop Laura from telling her friends about me, and of course if she told them about me, she'd have to mention how come we'd never met before. But it meant that more and more people were coming in on the secret. The lie was getting too big.

I tried not to think about it. Instead I took out of my bag the piece of paper Jen had given me. She'd written out the rough story of a play by someone called Caryl Churchill.

'We've been studying Caryl Churchill recently so I know all about it. Look at what

I've written on the train on your way home, then if your mum starts quizzing you, you'll know what you're talking about. Remember – I played the part of Betty.'

So I sat there trying to learn the plot of a play so I could build up a bit more deceit.

'Hi, love,' said Mum, leaning over to give me a kiss as I got into the car. 'Was it good?'

'Quite good,' I answered carefully, my heartbeat speeding up. 'Jen was fantastic, but I didn't understand the play all that well.'

'Yes, Caryl Churchill *is* very different, isn't she? I must say I was surprised that Matt and Jen thought you'd enjoy it.'

Mum's voice sounded a bit odd. I glanced at her out of the corner of my eye. She looked normal, except for a tiny muscle in her jaw that was twitching a bit.

'I think it was just because I'd been pestering to see Jen in something for so long.'

There was a pause, then Mum broke into a sudden smile. 'Well, now you have, haven't you? That's the main thing.'

We were quiet for the rest of the journey. I was thinking about how great the ten-pin bowling was and wishing I could tell Mum about it. If it had been Chloe's birthday I would have been full of it, and Mum would have been smiling away, asking me all sorts of questions.

When we were nearly home I asked her what she'd been doing.

'Dad and I have been gardening all day. I think you'll notice the difference!'

She turned her head quickly to give me a big smile, and my chest hurt for a second.

8 JEN'S COUSIN LAURA

Laura and I e-mailed each other on Monday
and Tuesday. Both e-mails were on the same
subject – what story we could invent so we
could get to see each other at the weekend. It
would have been much easier to work it out on
the phone, but more risky, and it would have
been too expensive to talk on our mobiles.

On Wednesday evening Laura sent me an
e-mail that started to change things.

Hi Katie,
I've just had a brilliant brainwave. I've

told Matt and Jen and they think it could work OK. How about telling your mum that you met Jen's cousin Laura when you saw the play, and that we really got on well and everything, then I can phone you and you can ask your mum if you're allowed to come to my house. That way you'd be telling the truth about everything except one thing. And she'll never find out about how you and I are related. Mum says she doesn't mind meeting you off the train. What do you think? Brill, eh?

Lots of love, Me.

The idea that Laura was Jen's cousin was very clever. Once I'd told that one small lie, everything else I said would be about the real Laura, so it would all be true.

I knew Mum was ironing in the kitchen and Dad was doing something or other in his little office, so I decided to go and talk to

Mum straight away, before the nervousness set in.

I'll pretend Laura's just e-mailed me! I almost burst out laughing. Laura *had* just e-mailed me, hadn't she?

'Mum,' I began, the moment I got through the kitchen door, 'I've just had an e-mail from Jen's cousin Laura.' My mouth felt a bit dry so I gabbled on quickly. 'We met last Saturday at Jen's play and we got on really well. She's the same age as me and she lives quite near to Matt and Jen's university. Anyway, she was wondering if I could go to her house at the weekend. So can I? She says if I come on the train, her mum'll pick me up from the station.'

'Slow down, darling,' smiled Mum. 'I can't say yes just like that. I'll have to talk to Dad about it, and also to Laura's mum.'

Laura's mum! Good job Mum was concentrating on the ironing. I didn't trust my face not to give the game away.

I mumbled 'OK' and started to creep out, but what Mum said next stopped me in my tracks. 'Why didn't you mention Laura on Saturday?'

I gulped. 'I just . . . didn't.' *Talk about a pathetic answer.*

'Hmm.' A little shadow went flitting across her face. 'I think it might be a better idea if Laura came here instead of you disappearing off again.'

'Yes . . . OK . . .'

But it wasn't OK, it was terrible. I couldn't let Mum meet Laura. That would be just shoving the lie right under her nose.

My heart plummeted down to the floor at Mum's next words. 'I'll talk to Dad, then I'll phone Laura's mum. What's her last name, by the way?'

'Erm . . . I don't know.'

Mum looked up from her ironing. She spoke quietly. 'But you've got her phone number?'

'No, we only exchanged e-mail addresses. I'll just phone Jen to ask her.'

But instead I went straight to my room and phoned Matt.

'Mum's going to phone Laura's mum!' I hissed urgently. 'What shall we do?'

'Blimey, you were quick off the mark. We only heard about the "Jen's cousin" plan half an hour ago.'

'Yeah, but what shall we *do*?' I knew I was jabbering. 'Mum wants Laura to come here instead of me going there.'

Matt sighed a big sigh, but what he said surprised me. 'She'll just have to come then. If you think about it, it's no worse than you going to Laura's. Either way Mum still thinks that Laura is Jen's cousin.'

'But she's going to phone Claire!'

'So what? Claire's not stupid. She'll say all the right things.'

It made me feel better hearing how calmly

Matt was taking it all. There was still one thing that was worrying me though. 'Mum asked me what Laura's last name is. I said I didn't know.'

It only took Matt a couple of beats. 'OK, let's settle on Marshall for the name. We're not likely to forget that. I'll phone Claire and warn her that Mum'll be phoning.' I could hear Jen's voice in the background but I couldn't make out what she was saying. 'Jen's just reminded me we were thinking of popping down on Sunday, so if you made it Sunday rather than Saturday we could bring Laura with us.'

'OK. Can you phone Claire straight away, before Mum does?'

'Yes.'

'And then can you phone Mum and tell her you're coming down on Sunday.'

'Yes. And Kates, you realise you're going to have to be extremely careful from now on, and especially on Sunday. *Think* before you speak.

If you let anything slip it'll be curtains for you. Well, curtains for all of us, actually.'

I shivered as I put the phone down.

'Hello, is that Mrs Marshall?' said Mum, about an hour later.

I was sitting opposite her at the kitchen table, trying to stop myself shaking.

I could just make out Claire's voice on the other end. 'Yes, it is.'

'My name's Julia Oriss. I gather our daughters have made friends.'

I heard Claire laugh and say something that contained the word 'Katie'.

Then Mum laughed too. 'I understand that my son's girlfriend is your niece?'

I didn't hear Claire's answer, partly because it was drowned out by my thumping heart. There was something scary about knowing an adult was telling lies.

'Anyway, I was wondering if Laura would

like to come and spend the day with us at the weekend. My son's just phoned to say that he and Jen are planning on popping down this Sunday, and I'm sure they wouldn't mind bringing Laura with them.'

Claire must have been saying that was fine, because a moment later Mum said, 'Lovely. I'll talk to Matt then.' I just about made out the word 'Jen' from Claire's end. 'That's a good idea.'

They said goodbye, and as Mum put the phone down I breathed a big sigh of relief.

'Laura's mum sounds very nice. She's going to phone Jen to sort out what time they'll pick Laura up.'

'Great!'

I think.

9 A CLOUD OF MIDGES

At eleven o'clock on Sunday morning I was walking round the house feeling the most nervous I've ever felt in my life. Part of it was excitement that Laura and I were going to have such a lot of time together, but most of it was fear of Mum meeting Laura. I couldn't stop thinking how awful it would be if Mum recognised her. But she couldn't. There was no chance. After all, Laura was Chris's daughter, not Martin's. All the same, I knew I'd feel better once Laura and Mum had got that first meeting over.

Matt's Citroën drew up at ten past eleven.

'Here they are!' said Mum, going to the front door to meet them.

We walked down the drive together in the spitting rain, as they were getting out of the car.

'Hi,' I said to Laura, smiling a bit shakily and trying to keep an eye on Mum.

Matt came straight round to give Mum a big hug. Then Dad appeared.

'Hello,' he said brightly. 'Don't like your choice of weather very much!'

It was a bit of an old joke of Dad's, but right now I was glad he'd made it, because everyone laughed.

'Come inside, all of you. I think the heavens are about to open,' said Mum, smiling at Laura.

I walked with Laura. We exchanged a look of *so far so good*.

'Good journey?' asked Mum as we all piled into the hall.

'Not bad,' said Matt. 'A few road works

about halfway here, but nothing major.'

'Not too much traffic then?' asked Dad.

'Very quiet, actually,' said Jen.

By then we'd got into the kitchen.

'Sit down. Let's have elevenses,' smiled Mum. I felt sorry for Laura. Mum's eyes were on her, and she'd gone a bit pink.

I tensed up.

A moment later everything was OK because Jen suddenly started sniffing the air with a jokey, suspicious look on her face. 'What's the smell, Julia?'

'Smell? I don't know. What kind of smell?'

'A lovely sort of woodland smell.'

'Yes, I can smell something too,' said Laura. 'Like blossom.'

'It's probably this pine table. I sprayed a bit of furniture polish on it this morning.'

Jen leaned forward and practically stuck her nose to the surface of the table. 'What do you reckon, Laura? Is this it?'

Laura had a sniff. 'Mmmm, lovely!'

Mum laughed. 'Glad you like it! Now what about something to drink?'

Afterwards, when I thought back to that moment, I guessed that Jen had deliberately distracted Mum's attention to lighten everything up. Then while the adults sat round having hot drinks, Laura and I bolted back our lemonade and went up to my room.

On the way upstairs, Laura said, 'Your mum's really good looking, isn't she?' I didn't have a chance to answer. 'I bet everyone says that, don't they?'

'I suppose . . .'

'You look more like her than like my grandfather. So does Matt. My dad looks like Grandpa though.'

'When did you last see . . . Martin?'

'Ages ago, but I've seen photos.' We went into my room. 'I've been trying to picture you when you're sending me e-mails, and now I can!' said Laura, looking round. 'You're very tidy, aren't you?' she added.

'I cleared up specially.'

'That's what *I* did when you came!' She sat on my bed and bounced up and down. 'Isn't it great that we don't have to be secretive any more?'

'I know! I can just ask Mum whenever I want to phone you!'

The moment the words were out of my mouth I had a sudden memory of something that happened when I was in year six, at the top of primary. Chloe, Emily, Mia and I always hung around together. But one day, Emily had to stay in at break to finish off some work and Chloe was away. I was sitting on the bench in the playground with Mia, when a really cool girl called Courtney asked me to come over and look at something. I remember glancing at Mia and feeling a little stab of pity because she wasn't being asked, only me. Then I told myself not to be silly. *You're only going to look at something. Katie. You'll be back in a minute.*

But I wasn't, because Courtney got me to join in their game, and it was a team game, and she said I wasn't allowed to drop out, otherwise the game would be spoilt. I asked if Mia could join in, and she said that that would make the teams uneven. I knew I ought to go back to Mia because she looked so sad, watching me from the bench, but I couldn't face the thought of everyone being cross if I did. So I suffered the game till the end of break, and then had a really hard time explaining to Mia that I'd wanted to get out of it but it had been impossible.

And now I had that very same feeling, only this time the stab of pity I felt was for Mum. She was the one on her own, and I was the one in the game. And the game was just too difficult to get out of.

Or was it? I wasn't in year six any more, was I?

A new thought came into my head – just a teeny idea fluttering around, wondering whether or not to stay and take root. Maybe it wouldn't be the very end of the world if I told Mum. She'd be terribly upset at first, of course, but then she'd realise that she liked Laura, and that Laura had nothing to do with Martin. And neither did Chris. I knew Chris and his father didn't get on and they never saw each other these days. Apparently Martin's partner, Dawn, is the same age as Claire. Chris and Claire had told me they found that a bit weird. So did I. Once Mum came to understand everything, she'd feel OK about it all. Surely.

'Laura?' She turned from looking at my CD covers. I decided to go carefully. 'I feel kind of sorry for Mum.'

She nodded with a sympathetic look on her face. 'It's a shame, isn't it?'

'I was thinking, maybe if I told her . . .'

She gasped and her eyes grew massive.

'Oh Katie, you can't do that now. You'd get everyone into trouble. Especially Matt!'

'I know it would be awful at first, but then once we'd got that bit over with it would be so much better. We could stop all the deceit –'

'But what if your mum was so angry that she refused to let you and me see each other any more? How bad would that be?'

'I don't think –'

She didn't let me finish. Her eyes were flashing. 'Whatever you do, Matt would never stop being friends with my dad, you know. He's a grown-up. He can do what he wants.'

It annoyed me the way she was telling me what my own brother would do. Part of me felt like arguing with her, but then I realised she was probably right. I'd just be making waves that would turn into a massive great breaker. I might as well leave it alone.

I nodded slowly and she gave me a quick hug. 'What shall we do?'

'Shall I phone Chloe and see if she can come over?'

'OK.'

But there was no reply from Chloe's house, and her mobile was on answerphone, so Laura and I went out for a walk. I showed her my old primary school (my secondary school was too far away to walk), then we looked round the few shops that were open and stopped in a Starbucks to have a coffee. Laura had a really frothy one and every time she took a sip she looked like she'd got a white moustache. I don't know why I found that so funny, but I did.

We passed the playground on the way home, and as there was no one around, decided to have a go on the slide. When I had my turn, Laura stood at the bottom pretending I was a toddler and she was my mother.

'That's right, darling!' she said, pursing her lips and sticking her arms out.

I was giggling so much I fell off the bottom, and when she'd heaved me back on my feet we both realised we had an audience. A real mother and toddler had turned up and the mother was giving us such a disapproving look that we thought we'd better get going. It was so painful trying to smother our laughter until we were well out of earshot.

'It's going to be a late lunch,' said Mum as we went in the kitchen at about two o'clock. She was giving us a mock cross look.

Dad tapped his watch and raised his eyebrows, but he was smiling.

I clapped my hand to my mouth. 'Sorry, Mum, we forgot all about the time.'

'Yes, sorry, Julia. Can we help?' asked Laura.

Mum gave her a radiant beam. She loves it when my friends are all polite and helpful. 'You could set the table if you like.'

'Where've you two been then?' asked

Matt, coming into the kitchen with Jen.

'Playing on the slide,' giggled Laura.

'Little things please little minds!' said Matt.

'No, sweetie, not at all,' said Jen. 'Slides are the most glorious fun!'

'Right, I think we're ready for take-off,' smiled Mum, bringing the roast over to the table.

'Mmm!' said Dad, going to his place. 'Smells good.'

'But first,' said Matt, looking a bit embarrassed, 'Jen's got something to tell you.'

'You big chicken, Matt Oriss! This is for *you* to tell!'

For a second I felt dizzy.

'OK, here goes,' said Matt. He pretended to be taking a very deep breath. 'Jen and I have got engaged.'

'Oh, wonderful!' said Mum, springing up from the table and clasping her hands together. 'Absolutely wonderful!'

'That's great news!' said Dad. 'Congratulations to both of you!'

Then Jen showed us her ring, and while Mum and Dad oohed and aahed, Laura and I sat there grinning. I don't know about Laura, but I was thinking that actually it wasn't such a big announcement. After all, they'd been acting like a married couple for ages. But then something hit me.

I leaned forwards and grabbed Matt's wrist. 'Can I be a bridesmaid?'

The moment my words were out in the open, if felt as though someone had opened the window and a cloud of midges had flown in. They didn't make a sound, just hovered horribly over the table. And every midge was a thought . . .

Wedding?

Guests.

Chris and Claire.

Secrets.

Lies.

A tiny slip from an innocent guest – 'No, it's Chris Marchant, *not Chris Marshall.'*

10 BEST MAN? BEST NOT!

The midges drifted away, leaving my question hanging in the air like a great big banner.

'Course you can, sweetie,' said Jen. 'It's going to be so fantab –'

Laura leaned forward, eyes shining. 'Can I, Matt?'

I gasped. She can't have been thinking. She was only supposed to be a cousin, *and* she'd asked Matt instead of Jen, by mistake.

There was a puzzled look on Mum's face.

'You'll have to ask Jen,' said Matt quickly.

'Absolutely, darling. You two will look

perfect together!'

Laura went a bit pink. She must have just realised her big mistake.

'Who's going to be the best man?' asked Dad.

Every muscle in my body seemed to tighten.

'Not decided,' said Matt. 'It won't be for ages yet, will it, Jen?'

'*Noooooo, nooooo!* Dim and distant future! I need oodles of time to work out the most theatrical wedding possible!'

I wondered if she was just saying that to get off the subject of best man.

'Oh no! What have I let myself in for?' said Matt, dropping his head dramatically into his hands.

Everybody laughed and the talk drifted on to the reception and where it would be held and all that. Laura and I didn't join in much. I knew she was as wrapped up in her thoughts as I was.

Best man? Chris? No, impossible. The lie would be too big to live with.

* * *

We all had brilliant fun playing board games till seven o'clock when Matt said that they'd better be making a move. Laura and I begged for a bit more time, but we knew we were on to a loser there. All four adults started talking about *Monday morning* as though a new world was about to begin and we needed to prepare for it big time.

'Thank you very much for having me,' said Laura to Mum and Dad.

Mum gave her a big hug. 'It's been lovely, dear. I hope you'll come again.'

'I'd love to,' said Laura. Then Dad hugged her too.

'I'll phone you in the week, Katie,' Laura called out as she got into the back of Matt's car. She gave me a very special look, and I knew that I'd be really upset if anything ever stopped us being friends. There was no way I could tell Mum and Dad who she really was. The wedding was ages away. We'd cross that bridge when we came to it. In the meantime, we'd just carry on as we were. Then nothing and no one would be upset.

They'd only been gone about five minutes when I got a text from Laura.

Your Mum & Dad R SO sweet & kind. Great day. Can't w8 till next time. LOL Laura.

I showed Mum the text while we were looking at the holiday brochures with Dad.

'Well, we think Laura's sweet too!' said Mum. 'And very well brought up – offering to help before lunch . . .'

'. . . and clearing away the plates without being asked,' Dad added.

'We were wondering about our holiday this year,' said Mum, a little hesitantly. 'There's no reason why Laura shouldn't come with us, if you like.' She put her glasses on to take a closer look at the hotels in Menorca.

I was taken aback. It had already crossed

my mind about Laura coming, but I'd never imagined Mum would mention it. 'Yes, that'd be good . . .'

'Just a thought,' said Mum. 'She'd fit in like one of the family,' she added.

I bit my lip. It was too difficult to concentrate on holiday brochures after that, because I couldn't stop thinking about the wedding. I mumbled something about getting my school bag ready, then went up to my room and texted Jen's phone. Matt would still be driving. I didn't feel like talking. I just wanted one simple question answered.

What about best man?

The reply came back almost immediately. *Matt will phone U later. LOL. J.*

Hmm. What did that mean? *As if I didn't know.*

I worked out that they'd be dropping Laura off in about an hour, then they'd be back at their flat twenty minutes later.

And sure enough, exactly an hour and twenty minutes later my mobile rang. I snatched it up and checked the number. Matt.

'I bet you've chosen Chris for best man, haven't you?' I launched in.

'In a nutshell, yes.'

'Oh Matt,' I started wailing. 'We'll have to tell Mum and Dad. It'll be impossible to keep it a secret at the wedding. I mean, you must have told your friends at university that you've got a half-brother, and they'll be coming to the wedding, won't they?'

'A few people know, yeah. I'll just have to make sure they keep their mouths shut, that's all.'

'But what about Jen's family? How are you going to explain the sudden appearance of this amazingly close friend and cousin called Laura?'

Matt was losing his cool. '*They'll* have to be warned too. There aren't many of them. It won't be a problem.' He snapped the next bit at me. 'Can you just stop thinking about it all the time, Katie? We'll sort it out.'

'How *can* I stop? It's all right for you. You don't live here.'

'You've got to try and be grown up about it.'

'I *am* being grown up. I'm the only who *is*!'

Matt's voice had a sort of hard edge to it that I'd never heard before. 'This wedding is very important to me and Jen, Katie. I know it's not for another year or so, but nothing, and I mean *nothing* is going to cock it up.'

'Well, you'd better tell Mum and Dad the truth then,' I said, feeling my temper rising, 'before I do.'

With that I disconnected and switched my phone off. I felt horrible and I knew Matt would be panicking, but I could feel this whole thing getting out of control, so why didn't anyone else?

Downstairs, Mum and Dad had chosen a holiday and were writing down a list of things to do the next day. I sat at the kitchen table and started reading the Sunday magazine, pretending I was absorbed in it, but really I was tuning in to what Mum and Dad were doing.

They were looking at each other's diaries, their heads close together. Why did everything always have to be so carefully planned? Why couldn't they do things impulsively like some of my friends' parents did? It must be because they were quite a bit older than my friends' parents. I looked at Mum's face. There were lots of fine lines on it, but she was still very good looking. And Dad looked like a bald owl, very kind and wise, with his high forehead and round glasses.

Why did it irritate me all of a sudden?

'Ready for school tomorrow?' Mum asked me.

What kind of a question was that? It made

me feel such a baby. I started slapping pages of the magazine over. That's what irritation does for you. Then I found myself wondering what would happen if I suddenly said, *By the way, did I tell you, Laura is actually Martin's granddaughter?*

A flood of nervousness came over me at the thought, but almost immediately it changed to anger. Why did I have to get myself all screwed up about something that wasn't even my problem? It was so unfair.

11 ANOTHER LINK IN THE CHAIN

Mia and Emily were at choir on Monday lunchtime, which gave me the perfect chance to tell Chloe all that had happened at the weekend. We sat in the cloakroom together.

'To think I was at some boring car boot sale!' said Chloe, hanging on to my every word. 'It would have been so much better if I'd been able to meet Laura.'

'You can definitely meet her the next time she comes down. I know you'll really like her. She's just the same as us – all normal and nice.'

Chloe laughed, then almost immediately

her face snapped back into seriousness again. 'The wedding's going to be a bit weird though, isn't it?'

'That's what *I* think, only Matt seems to think it'll be fine.'

'What does Laura think?'

'I'm not sure. We didn't have much time to talk about it. But I don't see how we can keep Mum in the dark any more.'

'What if you told her and it kind of drove her . . . mad?' Chloe was knitting her eyebrows together.

I stared at the floor. This was the very conversation that went on inside my head the whole time.

'But there again,' Chloe went on, with a thoughtful look in her eyes, 'if you think something strongly enough, you should go for it. Why not just tell your mum and have done with it?'

I couldn't believe what I was hearing. It

didn't matter how strongly *I* felt about it, the others had to feel the same. 'You're joking! I'd never say anything unless the others all agreed.'

'Why not?'

'Because of the wedding. I don't want to be the one to cock it up.'

Chloe nodded slowly. I could tell she wasn't convinced.

That evening Laura phoned, sounding really excited.

'Mum says it's OK for you to come over next weekend. Do you think you'll be allowed?'

In a split second I told myself that I'd worry about the big secret later, because I was so keen to go to Laura's. 'Cool! I expect so.'

'Do you want Mum to have a word with your mum?'

'Yeah, there's more chance of me being allowed that way.'

Mum was at the kitchen table, stapling

children's pictures on to coloured backing paper, ready to go up on the library wall at the primary school. 'It's Laura's mum,' I said, handing her the phone.

From this end it sounded like Mum was agreeing that I could go for the whole weekend. Wicked! But then, the next moment, it didn't sound quite so wonderful.

'No, no, Claire, I can easily come and collect her after lunch.' My heart missed a beat. 'Really, it's no trouble at all. I don't mind the drive in the slightest.'

After they'd finished talking, Mum handed me the phone and gave me a quick smile. Then she carried on stapling and I went upstairs.

'Isn't it so cool!' squeaked Laura. 'You're staying the night!'

'I know!' It was horrible of me to flatten her high spirits, but I couldn't help feeling anxious. 'What about Mum collecting me though?'

'What about it?'

Laura didn't seem bothered. Perhaps she hadn't thought it through. 'She'll see your dad. She might realise who he looks like.'

'Oh, Dad'll just have to go out or something. It'll be fine.'

Didn't Laura care? I suddenly flipped. 'He won't be able to go out at the wedding, will he?'

The moment the words were out of my mouth, I knew I shouldn't have spoken like that. It was the kind of thing I would have said to Matt, not to my new friend.

There was a pause. Laura sounded different. 'Yeah, Matt told me you'd had a go at him. He's not that happy with you.'

That did it. How dare Matt talk to Laura behind my back! I completely lost my temper. 'I couldn't care less. He can be as unhappy as he wants. He can't go on adding to the lies. The secret's too big to keep already, but by the time those two go up the aisle with Chris waiting at the front and you following behind, the whole thing'll explode! How come I'm the only one to see that?'

'Because you don't see things like we do. You've not been involved for as long as the rest of us.'

With that she disconnected, and I was left staring at the phone and trembling so much that I had to sit down on the bed.

Jen phoned about five minutes later. She was trying to be calm, but I could tell she was totally uptight.

'Look, love, Laura's really upset –'

'Well, how do you think *I* feel?'

'I know. I'm not excusing her. It's just that she's very sorry –'

'Why hasn't she phoned up and apologised then? Or has she got you to do it?'

Jen ignored that. 'Matt and I think you may have got a point about the secret getting too big.'

'At long last someone's listening to me!'

'So what we'd like to do, love – because it involves all of us now – is to get together this Saturday at Chris's place and talk it through.'

Later I checked my e-mail, and there was one from Laura, as I'd thought there might be.

> *I'm really really sorry if I upset you, Katie. My mum says you're much more involved with everything than I am, and that it's no wonder you can't stand the secret because you have to live with it all the time. Open the attachment now!*
> *LOL, Laura XX*

So I opened the attachment and it was a special sorry card with music. I didn't know you could get sorry cards on e-mail – I'd only ever seen birthday cards before. It was really sweet and a lovely surprise. I stared at it for a while, thinking ahead to the weekend.

Another link to add to the chain of lies.

12 THE PRETENCE MUST GO ON

Laura and I spotted each other at opposite ends of the platform at exactly the same moment. We both broke into a jog. It was awkward for me because of my bag banging against my hip. But as we drew nearer, she stuck her arms out and started running in slow motion, pretending we were playing a really old-fashioned love scene. I could feel a big fit of giggles welling up inside me as I did the same. People must have been staring at us, but I didn't care. The funniest thing of all was that when Laura was almost level with me she veered off to the side and went straight past me.

We were still killing ourselves as we left the platform and walked across the car park. Claire was leaning on her car. 'I can see this is going to be a pretty hysterical weekend,' she called out, shaking her head slowly.

Laura grabbed my wrist. 'Let's get into the back. We can pretend we're in a taxi.'

The journey back to their house was totally mad, because we were both being so childish, acting the parts of very posh women who had nothing to do but shop all day and could afford a private chauffeur. I could see through the driving mirror that Claire was smiling to herself as we pretended to put on lipstick and do our hair, but I guessed she was used to Laura's sense of humour.

'Guess what,' said Laura, as we got out of the car at her house. 'We're going for a Chinese tonight – all of us.'

For a moment I thought she was still in her posh woman role, and I laughed and said,

'Soooooper, darling! But couldn't we make it Japanese?'

Laura cracked up. 'No, really, Katie. Mum and Dad, Matt and Jen, you and me – we're all going.'

'Oh. Right.'

We'd been in another little world where everything was a joke, but now we were back to reality, I didn't like the feeling. I might have been imagining it, but it seemed to me that the others had all been talking without me. I wondered whose idea it was to go for a Chinese. I could just hear Matt . . .

Katie loves Chinese food. Let's go out for a meal – that'll put her in a good mood.

I couldn't get this thought out of my head all day, so although Laura and I had a good time, it would have been better without that cloud hanging over me. We spent the rest of the morning playing interactive games on the telly and listening to music.

After lunch we went shopping with Claire and Chris. While they went off to look at sofas, Laura and I tried on a few clothes in our favourite shops. I don't know what it is about the two of us being together in public places, but the tiniest thing makes us crack up. In Top Shop we had such a hysterical fit of the giggles that we had to leave the changing room because people were giving us funny looks.

Matt and Jen arrived at the Chinese restaurant about ten minutes after us. Loads of heads turned as Jen breezed in, smiling and sparkling. She was wearing a shiny miniskirt, a very short, tight top, ankle boots, a long scarf and massive earrings. She looked brilliant. Matt looked as scruffy as ever.

'What *is* she doing with him?' I whispered under my breath to Laura. Claire must have heard me because she sniggered.

'Terrible news!' squealed Jen, plopping

herself into the seat that Chris and Laura had left between them. 'We haven't got a bean between us, and we've both forgotten our credit cards.' She did praying hands to Claire. 'Pay you back tomorrow? Double promise!'

Claire laughed and Matt rolled his eyes. 'I thought we agreed to tell them at the end of the meal, not the beginning!'

'Oops!' said Jen. 'Sorry! Forget I spoke! Rewind! Pass us one of those menus, darling – I'm starving!'

'The things we do for you two,' said Chris, shaking his head.

'It's because he's your brother,' said Laura. '*And* your best friend.'

'I don't know about that,' said Chris.

'You must be best friends, Dad, otherwise Matt wouldn't have chosen you for best man at his wedding, would he?'

There was a short silence while everyone shuffled about in their seats.

Laura mouthed 'sorry' to her mum, so I knew I was right. They *had* been talking behind my back.

I glared at Matt.

'OK, let's order the food then talk about *the problem*,' he said, sounding completely hacked off.

'Good plan, babe,' said Jen, trying to keep everything light.

Claire gave a nervous little laugh, but everyone else's eyes were glued to their menus.

Once the orders were out of the way and the waiter had gone, Chris turned directly to me. The others immediately stopped talking and sat very still, hanging on to his every word.

'When Matt first got in touch with me and Claire, it was because he wanted to meet his half-brother. If he could have done that with your mum's blessing, then he would have. He knew he couldn't, and he didn't want to upset her, so he decided to keep it a secret. He had no idea – and neither did we at that stage – that we'd get so close. But you can't stop these things from happening. Same with Matt and Jen – they didn't know they were going to get married when they first met each other. Same with you – you didn't know that you and Laura were going to hit it off really well. So we can't all sit here and look at the situation we have right now and say *We were wrong not to have told your mum before*, because before was before and now is now. Things have changed.'

I heard Claire say 'Mmm,' very quietly. Other than that, there wasn't a murmur round the table. I didn't want to look, but I guessed all eyes were on me to see how I was taking the big speech.

Chris carried on. 'When Jen and Matt get married, they want a really special day. Their parents will want that too – it's an important occasion to them. Matt and Jen are stuck in a big dilemma. They want me for best man and you two for bridesmaids. Apart from that, all they want is for everyone to be happy on that day. Now, this is the tough bit. You've heard the expression *Ignorance is bliss*. Well, that's what we're working on here. We can pretty well guarantee everyone else's happiness on the big day, but not your mum's. We all understand that she has her reasons for not wanting you and Matt to have anything to do with me or my father, so we need to make the best of the situation. And that means keeping her in the dark for her own protection, her own happiness, her own peace of mind . . .'

I'd listened for long enough. It was my turn now.

I knew what I felt, but I didn't know how to put it into words. 'But – but you don't live with her, Chris. You can't feel how big the lie is, like I can.'

There was a silence after I'd spoken. Jen wrinkled her nose. 'She's got a point, you know.'

Matt turned to me. His eyes were flashing. 'OK, let's just say you *do* tell her, and she completely flips – which she will – and forbids you to have anything more to do with Laura. What do you do then? Keep the friendship going behind her back? Because *that* would be much more deceitful than what we're all doing at the moment, you know.'

I had to admit he was right. For a moment I felt like bursting into tears because it seemed like everyone was ganging up on me.

Jen suddenly leaned forward and held my hand in both of hers. 'Tell you what, angel, why don't we compromise? Keep shtum until the wedding's over, then do what ever you feel is right. How about that?'

The others all made murmuring noises to show that they thought that was a good plan. Laura put her arm round my shoulder, and it was weird, but everything kind of shifted around in my head. I suddenly felt all wrapped up and safe in my new family, wishing Mum wasn't causing us so many problems. There was one other thing though . . .

'What if Mum recognises Chris?'

Claire cleared her throat. 'Yes, I've thought about that too, but I reckon it's only the beard and the hair that make him look like Martin – and he can change that.'

I nodded and felt suddenly tired of talking about it. I flopped back in my chair, and for some unknown reason Chloe's words came springing into my mind: *if you think something strongly enough you should go for it.*

Did I feel it strongly enough? No, not any more. Chris and the others were right. It would be tough, but the pretence had to go on, at least till after the wedding.

13 ENTER GRANNY MARYON

Laura and I made breakfast in bed for us two and for Chris and Claire next morning. When we'd flicked all the toast crumbs from Laura's bed into the bin, we went downstairs and watched a video. It was raining hard outside so we didn't do much else all morning, apart from helping to make lunch.

'What time is your mum coming to collect you?' Claire asked me casually, when we were peeling vegetables and Laura was buried in the deep-freeze looking for her favourite pudding.

'Er . . . somewhere round four o'clock, I think.'

'Right.' I could tell there was something else she wanted to say. 'Your mum might be curious about Jen and Laura being cousins, and it's important that we all stick to the same story. So we reckon it's best if we say that Chris is Jen's mum's much younger brother . . .' Claire must have seen the panic on my face, because she went on, 'Don't worry, you can just say you're not sure what the connection is, if she asks you.'

'I'm still worried that she might see a likeness between Chris and Martin.'

Chris came into the kitchen at that moment, bang on cue. 'How's it look?' he asked, grinning all over his face.

I gasped. He'd shaved off his beard and brushed his hair forwards.

Laura came rushing in from the utility room. 'Oh Dad! You look awful!'

'Well, thanks for the vote of confidence!'

'Never mind. At least you don't look anything like Grandpa now.'

'That's true,' smiled Claire.

I felt sick. It was so horrible that all this was happening to deceive Mum. But a second later my guilt had switched to anger again. It was her own fault. She shouldn't have put everyone in this position.

Claire turned brightly to Laura. 'So what have you chosen for pud, darling?'

Lunch was rather an odd meal. Everyone was being falsely cheerful. It was to cover up the tension, but it wasn't working.

Afterwards we cleared away quietly. Claire kept looking round the house, as though there might be some incriminating piece of evidence that needed to be hidden before Mum arrived. Laura and I cleaned out the rabbits' hutch then went and listened to music in her room.

It was a relief when the doorbell finally rang at just after four o'clock. Claire cleared her throat as she went to open it. Anyone would think she was about to make a speech. I followed nervously behind her.

'Hi, Mum. Oh, hi, Dad! I didn't know you were coming too.'

'Mum wasn't feeling a hundred per cent, so she got the old man to drive,' laughed Dad.

'Hello,' said Claire, shaking hands with Mum. 'Come in, both of you.' Then she looked really concerned. 'What a shame you're not feeling too good. Can I get you anything?'

'No, don't worry. It's just a headache and I've taken some aspirin, but they don't seem to be working.'

Dad and Claire introduced themselves as they shook hands, and I crossed my fingers behind my back. So far, so good. But where was Chris?

'Take Julia and Richard through to the

sitting room, Laura, and I'll put the kettle on,' smiled Claire.

She scurried off and left us to it.

'So what have you two been up to?' asked Dad as we all sat down.

We didn't get the chance to answer because Chris came in at that moment. Laura's eyes grew wide. I expect mine were the same. Chris kind of plunged across the room and grabbed Mum's hand and started pumping it. 'Hello. It's lovely to meet you.' Then he did the same to Dad, who'd jumped to his feet. 'How was your journey? Did you manage to find us OK?'

I was holding my breath and watching closely. Mum seemed to be acting normally, but it was difficult to tell because she was paler than usual and her eyes looked strained.

'No problems at all,' smiled Dad. 'Very good directions from Claire.'

'Mum's got a headache,' I blurted out. 'That's why Dad drove.'

'Oh, I'm sorry to hear that,' said Chris.

Then Claire appeared with a tray of cups and saucers, plates and biscuits. 'I'll just get the teapot. Can you offer round the biscuits, Laura?'

A few minutes later, when we were all drinking tea, I started to relax, because Mum was smiling and chatting, and not staring at Chris or anything. Laura nudged me and gave me a subtle thumbs-up. I didn't like her doing that. Not with Mum actually sitting there.

'So Laura and Jen are cousins?' Mum asked Claire brightly.

Claire darted Chris a quick look. 'Yes, Chris and Jen's mum are brother and sister.'

Mum nodded slowly, putting a hand to her forehead.

'Are you sure I can't get you anything for your head?' asked Claire, sympathetically.

'No, I'd better leave it a little longer,' said Mum. She laughed. 'Sorry, I'm not usually like this.'

'I get headaches when there's a storm brewing,' said Chris.

Dad was opening his mouth to speak when the doorbell rang.

Claire whizzed off, looking anxious. 'Who can that be?'

'I've got a friend at school who gets headaches from eating dark chocolate,' said Laura.

Then the door opened and in walked a bent old lady with bow legs.

'This is my grandmother,' said Claire, rolling her eyes at Chris.

'Hello, Granny Maryon,' said Laura loudly. Then she lowered her voice and added, 'She's deaf as a post. You have to shout.'

Granny Maryon didn't look to right or left, just marched up to the sofa and plonked herself down between Laura and Dad. She puffed a bit then said, 'Brrr. Nippy out.'

I was sitting on the floor next to Laura so I

had a good view of Granny Maryon's legs. She looked as though she'd got two pairs of tights on, but it might have been just one extra-thick pair. Her feet were swelling over the tops of her shoes.

'Let me introduce you, Granny,' Claire shouted. 'This is Laura's friend, Katie.'

Granny Maryon leaned forwards to look at me. 'Katie, d'you say?'

I nodded and smiled.

'Nice smile,' she said, showing her own false teeth. 'And do you go to Laura's school?'

'No, I'm just a friend.' I knew I was going pink, and I also knew Mum was looking at me.

'These are Katie's parents, Julia and Richard,' Claire carried on shouting out the introductions.

Granny Maryon didn't even glance at Mum and Dad. She just kept staring at me. 'You remind me of someone,' she said, her eyes narrowing.

My heart started thumping and I looked to Claire for help.

'What about a cup of tea, Granny?' she said, crouching down beside the old lady and holding one of her hands. Very slowly the beady eyes left my face and moved round to Claire's. My whole body heaved a massive sigh of relief, but it wasn't easy trying not to let it show.

'No tea for me dear. I'm on a mission.'

'A mission!' laughed Claire, probably as relieved as me that the conversation was changing.

Granny Maryon leaned back so she could pat her coat pocket with a bony hand. 'Brought you the raffle tickets from Mrs Carr.'

'Oh, lovely,' said Claire.

'I don't know what's lovely about it,' said Granny Maryon. 'Nothing but a bind, having to pester folk to buy them.'

'What are they in aid of?' asked Mum politely.

'The Lifeboats.'

'So you won't have a cup of tea then, Granny?' It was so obvious Claire wanted to get rid of her outspoken old granny.

But she wasn't about to go. The beady eyes swivelled back round to me again. 'So who did you say you were?'

'She's very confused,' Claire explained to everyone in an undertone. Then she turned the volume up again. 'Katie's a friend of Laura's, Granny.'

'She stayed over last night,' shouted Laura. 'And we had breakfast in bed!'

'What? Last night?'

'No, this morning.'

'Breakfast in bed!' said Dad. 'Snap! Me too.'

'Right, I'll be off then,' said Granny Maryon. Claire and Chris exchanged a look of relief. 'I'll leave you these raffle tickets on the hall table, dear. Don't worry about seeing me out.' She heaved herself up with a bit of help from Chris and headed purposefully for the door. 'Nice to meet you all. Ta-ra!'

Claire and Chris grinned at each other. Laura let a splutter of laughter escape, which instantly made me want to crack up. Mum didn't look quite as strained as she'd looked at first, and Dad was smiling broadly. But no sooner had the old lady gone out than she popped her head back round the door and wagged her finger at me. 'I've got it! I know exactly who you remind me of now!'

The gnarled old finger moved slowly round the room and stopped when it was in line with Chris. Then Granny Maryon stabbed the air triumphantly. 'Him!'

A rush of terror hit me in the gut.

Chris broke into loud, rather gulpy laughter. 'Poor Katie! It's not exactly a compliment, Granny Maryon. I should get going quick before she bites your head off!'

Dad burst out laughing, Claire and Laura

giggled nervously, but Granny Maryon was not amused. 'You shouldn't have shaved your beard off, Chris, then you wouldn't look so girlie!'

There was a loud silence, then Claire started ushering the old lady out. 'Come on, Granny.'

I risked a glance at Mum. She was rubbing the side of her forehead. 'I think I'll say yes to that aspirin, Chris, if you don't mind,' she said quietly.

Laura jumped up. 'I'll get them.'

'Poor Mum,' I said, my heart still booming away.

She gave me a weak smile and Dad said perhaps we ought to be making a move.

14 A CLOSED CHAPTER REOPENED

In the car Dad asked me what Laura and I had been up to during the weekend and I burbled on about going into town and watching the video. And all the time I was gabbling away, I kept on wishing that Mum would join in the conversation.

She just sat there, her head back against the headrest. I could see through the wing mirror that her eyes were closed. If only I could get inside her mind and find out what she was thinking. I was desperately clinging to the hope that her silence was because of her headache and not because – it was an unbearable thought – Granny Maryon's words had got her wondering.

When we ran out of conversation Dad put Radio 4 on. I don't know what the programme was about, except that it was extremely boring. I closed my eyes and after a few minutes found myself drifting off to sleep.

Next thing I knew, we were pulling into our drive.

'Here we are!' said Dad brightly.

I shot awake immediately and sat bolt upright, expecting to see Mum with a terrible grave look on her face. But, incredibly, she was back to her normal self. She swivelled round in her seat and smiled at me. 'I wonder what time *you* went to bed last night, young lady! You've been asleep practically the whole way.'

I was so relieved. Everything was all right after all! She didn't know our secret. Granny

Maryon hadn't blown it for us. 'Has your headache completely gone, Mum?'

'Yes, I'm feeling miles better, thanks. And I'm starving! Who fancies a takeaway?'

'Brill!'

So we went inside and phoned the Kebab House in town.

Chloe grabbed me the second I walked into the classroom on Monday morning. 'Did you have a great time? What happened with your mum?'

'Let's go the loos and I'll tell you on the way. I don't want anyone else to hear.' We nipped out into the corridor and I broke into a gabble about Mum being off colour, Chris shaving his beard off, and Granny Maryon turning up out of the blue and putting both her big swollen feet right in it.

Chloe hung on to my every word as I told her about the journey home, the tense silence,

Radio 4 and me falling asleep. Twice she bumped into people walking in the opposite direction, because she wasn't looking where she was going.

'So what happened when you woke up?'

'We were home and Mum was all better! I mean, she was completely back to her normal self. So it was obviously just her headache making her feel lousy. Thank goodness!'

'Hmm.' Chloe had suddenly stopped walking and was staring at the ground.

'What?'

Now she was really frowning. 'How do you know she was completely back to normal? How can you be sure it was just the headache making her like that?'

'It's obvious, isn't it? Because if she'd guessed our secret, she would have gone completely mad.'

'How do you know?'

What! Why was Chloe asking me these

ridiculous questions when we'd been over and over this ground loads of times? I looked round and suddenly realised we were the only people in the corridor.

Her next words seemed to bounce off the walls and hit me in the face. 'Just because she goes mad at the *thought*, it doesn't mean she'd go mad at the real thing.'

'B-but . . . she'd say something, wouldn't she? Not just carry on as normal?'

'Maybe she's waiting for *you* to say something first.'

This time Chloe had gone too far. She'd wound me right up and I'd had enough of the whole topic of conversation. 'I'm going back to the classroom. It'll be registration in a minute.'

After school I walked home instead of getting the bus. It took me ages, but I wanted to be on my own to think. Chloe's words were still booming in my head, driving me mad. Surely she was talking rubbish. But what if she wasn't? And how could I ever possibly find out?

I let myself in through the back door. Mum was studying a school-book catalogue.

'Hello, darling,' she smiled up at me. 'Good day?'

'Yeah, fine.'

'Look at this,' she said, holding out a tatty bit of paper.

I leaned over and read the smudged, misspelled words.

I fink bears are stupid but some people like them, so it duzent matter if you want to get them books you was on about. From Oz.

I giggled. 'Who's Oz, Mum?'

'Oscar Daley. He's absolutely obsessed with bears, but he thinks it's babyish and he doesn't want anyone to know. He left his little message tucked into this page of my catalogue, where all the bear books are listed. I've only just found it!'

Mum and I couldn't stop reading and re-reading the cute little note.

'What a child,' laughed Mum. 'Isn't it amazing the lengths he's gone to, to make sure I order those books! I wonder why he didn't just tell me.'

She was chuckling away as she went outside to get the washing in. I watched her face carefully, looking for clues. There were none. She definitely hadn't sussed anything at all. I *knew* I'd been right, all along. *Gutted Chloe*!

Later I found an e-mail from Laura.

> *Hi Katie,*
> *Thanks for the text message. Big relief that the secret's still safe! Phew! Matt and Jen came round after you'd gone. We all had a laugh about Granny Maryon and the close shave! Mum says G.M.'s not the mad old lady she might seem to be. Scary eh?*
> *Seeya, L.*

* * *

Without even thinking about it, I reached for the right mouse button and deleted the message. Then I shut down the computer and stared at the blank screen. The e-mail had disturbed me. I couldn't bear to think of them all sitting round laughing about something that wasn't funny at all. It was deadly serious – a closed chapter in Mum's life. And what had we done? Reopened it behind her back. Then sat round laughing when she'd nearly found out from an old lady. It was so unfair, so cruel. I had to stop it.

And once again those words of Chloe's came crashing into my mind. *If you think something strongly enough, you should go for it.*

I stood up abruptly and went downstairs.

Mum was humming to a song on the radio as she set up the ironing board. I stood by the door, my heart thumping so much it hurt my ribs. 'I've got something to tell you.'

She switched off the radio. 'Come and sit down.'

I felt as though I was sleep-walking . . .

. . . and sleep-talking. 'You know . . . Martin's got a son . . .'

She was nodding very slowly but her eyes were completely blank – not angry, not sad, not wondering, not worrying, not anything.

I gulped and thought about that e-mail. 'Well, you know Chris?'

Just more slow nods.

I was nearly there. 'Well, he's Martin's son.'

I'd said it. I clung to the seat of my chair and stared at the table and waited . . .

'I know.'

She'd spoken in a whisper. I must have misheard. My head shot up.

'You . . . know?'

'Granny Maryon left those raffle tickets for Claire in an envelope on the hall table. On the front it said Claire Marchant.

When I saw that, I knew for certain.'

I gasped. 'You knew for certain? You mean you'd already guessed?'

Mum breathed deeply. 'About a year ago when Matt came home for the weekend I checked his jeans pockets just before I put them in the wash, and I found a ticket printed with the name of some event or other, and underneath the words *Speaker – Chris Marchant*. I didn't think it was likely to be a coincidence.'

'Oh Mum!' I couldn't say any more. My throat was hurting too much.

Tears had come into her eyes. 'I've been waiting for Matt to tell me, but he never did.'

'He didn't dare. He thought you'd go mad.'

'That's what Dad said. Then when this cousin of Jen's appeared, I guessed you were in on the secret too, and I started waiting again. Dad said I was making it too hard for you. He said I shouldn't have reacted so aggressively when you brought it up recently. But I can't help how I feel.'

'So didn't you really have a headache yesterday? Were you just . . . upset?'

'No, love. I did have a headache, because I'd got myself into such a terrible state about meeting my stepson. I knew I had to confront this barrier of mine, but I was dreading it. I'd never really known Chris, you see.'

'Didn't he ever come and visit you and Martin before Martin left?'

Mum closed her eyes then opened them again. 'He was very angry with Martin for leaving him, and he refused to come to see him at our house. Then he went away to university and during the holidays he lived with his mother. If Martin wanted to see Chris he used to have to go round there.'

'So you'd never seen him before yesterday?'

Mum nodded slowly. 'Yes, just once, but I recognised him easily from Martin. The worst thing of all, though, was knowing that I had still longer to wait until you or Matt told me the truth. It's not been easy pretending that I didn't know what was going on. But it was important to me to keep up the pretence, because I didn't want you to be forced into a position where you *had* to tell me. I wanted you to *want* to tell me. I know it's stupid –'

'No, it's not!' I drew my chair closer to Mum's and put my arm round her, because she was nearly crying.

'It's all right,' she said, wiping her eyes. 'These aren't tears of sadness. I'm just so relieved that you've told me at last.'

And that's how we were when the door opened, and Matt walked in. His eyes looked enormous in his white face.

It was as though I'd seen a ghost. 'It's Monday! What are you doing here?'

He looked at Mum and spoke in barely

more than a croak. 'I thought . . . it was time we talked.' The croak faded to a whisper. 'But I see Katie's already started.'

'Yes, she's a brave girl,' Mum laughed through her tears.

'I know,' said Matt shakily. He came over and put an arm round both of us, leaned his head on Mum's head, then sat down opposite us. 'I've been driving far too fast for the last fifty minutes, and still I'm too late.'

'Only a year,' smiled Mum. 'What made you suddenly change your mind?'

Matt started gnawing at his thumb, which was what he used to do when he was nervous just before exams. 'Chris.'

'Chris!'

He went a bit red, but managed to look Mum in the eyes. 'Jen and I went round to Chris and Claire's last night. They told us what had happened with Granny Maryon and everything. But later, after Laura had gone to bed, Chris went very quiet. We all knew something was the matter. In the end he said he was sorry but he didn't think he could be best man at our wedding after all. We were gobsmacked and asked him why, and he said he hadn't minded keeping the secret from you until he met you properly, but everything had changed now and he thought Katie was right – it was time we were honest with you. And if you couldn't cope when you heard our secret, then that was that. We'd all have to take the consequences.'

It was ages before Mum spoke. 'What's their phone number again?'

Matt looked as horrified as I felt, but he told her the number, then motioned me to come out of the kitchen with him. We sat in the sitting room, talking softly about everything. It was the first time for ages that I'd felt as though Matt and I were having a proper conversation, on a level with each other.

'I have to hand it to you, Kates – you got it right. You really did.'

I smiled. It was nice to be complimented like that by Matt, but somewhere deep inside, I reckoned it was Chloe who'd got it right. I hadn't been able to get her words out of my head: *Maybe she's waiting for you to say something first.* I drew my knees up and hugged them. I couldn't wait to tell her that I'd done it.

15 GOING WITH THE FLOW

I was sitting right under the speaker, but I
didn't care that the music was pounding in my
ears. I was exhausted from dancing non-stop
for the last half-hour. My beautiful ivory-
coloured dress was beginning to look like a rag.
I glanced across at Laura, who was dancing
with Dad and Claire. Her dress looked pretty
bedraggled too. My eyes roamed round the
whole room and the lovely happiness I'd been
feeling all day kept bubbling away inside me.

Jen was dancing a slow dance with Matt,
even though the music was fast and pounding,

and everyone else was going wild. The two of them were lost in a little married world of their own. She looked absolutely beautiful, even if she was wearing the most off-beat bridal gown in the history of man. 'I'm going to reverse the concept, darlings,' she'd said to Laura and me when she'd showed us what we were all going to be wearing on the big day. 'I want the bridesmaids to look utterly traditional in pure white, silky dresses, and the bride – that's me, lovies – in more of a rainbow creation. You know how I've always loved that grunge look.'

'Oh Jen, you can't!' we'd giggled. But we were secretly hoping she would, because, as she'd kept saying, it was going to be 'fab, sweeties!'.

Mum and *her* mum had got together and persuaded her to rethink the white and have ivory for the bridesmaids, but they hadn't been able to persuade her to tone down her own dress. The top was tight, sleeveless and silver, with a high neck and a big hole in the back. It clung down to her hips then flared out and swirled and glistened with slim panels of blues and violets whenever Matt spun her round. She'd also dyed her hair purple and blue for the occasion.

I grabbed my camera and took a close-up of the loving couple. They didn't even notice the flash.

Dad and Jen's dad were just behind me. They were shaking their heads at the sight of Jen.

'It's like tennis and cricket,' I heard her dad say to mine. 'The youngsters have lost all sense of tradition, haven't they?'

'You're not wrong there, Peter!'

I glanced across the room. Mum and Chris were still deep in conversation. Chris was leaning forward and trying to explain something to her. He was drawing big arcs in the air. Mum was smiling and nodding. It was incredible the way the two of them got on. I found myself going back to that day when Matt and Mum and I had sat white-faced round the table, and Mum had asked for Chris's phone number. I'll never know what they said to each other on the phone. All I know is that Dad had come back from work in the middle of it, and when Matt and I told him who Mum was talking to, he let his breath out really slowly, flopped into a chair and said, *At long last*.

Mum had come off the phone wreathed in smiles, grabbed Dad and said, 'Come on – we're going to meet Chris in The Bull at Crayton. It's about halfway.'

Dad had winked at Matt and me as he'd gone rushing out after Mum, who was already getting in the car.

Since that evening, she and Dad had met up with Chris and Claire quite a bit and they were all really good friends now. I was still good friends with Laura too, but we didn't see each other all that often. My best friend would always be Chloe – and talking of Chloe, where was she? I looked round and spotted her coming back from the loos.

'Chlo! Over here!'

She grinned and ran over, shaking her mobile at me and looking excited. 'I've just been talking to Mia, telling her how brilliant it is.'

'Don't you mean fantab?'

Chloe laughed. 'Mia thought Jen's dress sounded pretty fantab!'

'I heard Jen's grandfather grumbling away about it to Granny Maryon. They didn't realise I was listening.'

'What did Granny Maryon say?'

'She told him to wake up to the twenty-first century and go with the flow!'

'She really is an amazing old lady, isn't she?'

I nodded, and we both looked at her

grinning away and clapping in time to the music.

Then my eyes drifted over to Matt and Jen. 'Do you realise, Chlo, those two have slow-danced to every single record, even the fast ones?'

Chloe laughed. Then she hunched up her shoulders like an excited little girl. 'I can't wait till this time next week, Kate!'

'Me neither. Is that your phone ringing again?'

After Chloe had gone rushing out to talk to Emily, I had another look round. Mum was sitting with Granny Maryon and Chris was dancing with Claire. Laura was talking to some university friends of Jen's.

'Come and talk to us, Katie,' Granny Maryon called out.

Mum squeezed my hand as I sat down between the two of them.

'Are you enjoying the party, Granny Maryon?'

'Yes I am, thank you, dear.' She stuck her glass out to a passing waiter. 'Are you doing top-ups, young man?'

The man was at least forty but he smiled at her and said he was.

'I'll have another of those Bacardi Browsers – they're very nice indeed.'

'Another Bacardi Breezer? Certainly, Madam.'

'I might get the name wrong, but I know how to knock 'em back!' chuckled Granny Maryon as the waiter went off with her glass.

Mum and I agreed that she certainly did.

'I'll let you into a little secret,' she went on. 'On my ninetieth birthday I said to myself, *Maryon, you've been leading a good clean safe life, obeying all the rules for ninety years. How boring! Isn't it about time you started to live a bit?*'

Mum and I cracked up laughing.

'But you see, my dears, it's not as funny as you may think. I was brought up to be careful and tactful and considerate and obedient. All very fine principles, but since my ninetieth birthday I've been throwing caution to the wind and hanging loose! And do you know, I've found it's improved my life considerably!' She chuckled. 'In fact, it's improved other people's lives too. I mean, where would you be now, Julia, if I hadn't come out with that ridiculous comment when I first met you and Katie at Claire's?'

'What ridiculous comment?' Mum asked slowly.

'You know – pretending that Katie reminded me of Chris,' she said, beaming at us.

Mum and me turned big eyes on each other, then looked back at Granny Maryon.

'You mean –'

'So you never –'

'You were just –'

'Absolutely!' said Granny Maryon. 'Got it in one! I merely wanted to stir things up so you could sort yourselves out. Claire and Chris imagine I'm completely gaga, but I've got eyes and ears and I've also got a terrible tendency to snoop.' She laughed. 'I'd known that Matt and Chris were brothers for a long time before I met you.' And with that, she leapt up and grabbed her Bacardi Breezer from the smiling waiter who'd just appeared. 'I was wondering, young man, do your duties extend to dancing with old ladies?'

The waiter looked shocked and began stuttering, but Granny Maryon slapped the drink down on the table, grabbed his hand and led him on to the dance floor. Then the whole room began clapping and cheering.

Mum turned and looked me in the eyes. 'Isn't it incredible how things have changed?'

'Yeah, but some things never change,' I answered. 'The new bits kind of slot in, but the old bits stay the same.'

'That's a nice way of putting it, Katie.

I suppose you're thinking about Chloe, aren't you?'

I nodded, happy that she'd picked up on it so quickly. 'I can't wait till we go away next week.'

'It's going to be a wonderful holiday. You were right to choose Chloe, not Laura.' She smiled. 'I only suggested Laura when we were looking at those brochures, to give you the chance to tell me about her if you wanted to.'

I bit my lip. 'I didn't dare.'

Mum put her hand on top of mine. 'It's OK. You made it right in the end, didn't you? Granny Maryon might have churned things up a little bit, but it was you who made it right.'

'Come on, sweeties!' cried Jen. 'Everyone on the dance floor!'

I leapt up and thought Mum was following, but when I turned round she was deep in conversation with her stepson.

'Not again!' I said quietly and happily to myself.

Dad heard me though. 'They've got a lot of catching up to do, you know.'

I rolled my eyes. 'I know.'

'Come on,' he said. 'Come and have a dance with your old dad.'

So I did.

What happens next in the step-chain?
Meet Ashley in . . .

Step-Chain

HEALING THE PAIN

1 THE CONSPIRACY

Granny's loud voice cut in on my thoughts. 'I said do you want another cup of tea, Ashley?'

I dragged myself back to earth and shook my head. 'No thanks, Gran.'

She was giving me one of her searching looks. 'You're always daydreaming these days, young lady. Don't you get told off at school?'

I shrugged. 'Not really.'

The truth was I couldn't help daydreaming. There were so many horrible thoughts bugging me – thoughts about Ben, and when I'd first changed my mind about him. It was so brilliant at the beginning, when he and Mum started going out with each other. Mum stopped being tired and snappy all the time, and started being really good fun.

Kieran and I didn't actually see that much of her, because when she wasn't working at the hospital she was going out with Ben, but we weren't bothered because Mum was happy. Anyway, we'd got Granny. She'd been living with us for years – ever since Dad moved out.

But then gradually Mum and Ben stopped going *out* so much and started staying in together. And next thing we knew he was coming round here even when Mum was at work. I didn't mind at first, but after a while it started to get on my nerves, because he was always poking his nose into things that were nothing to do with him, and kept on asking us questions, like he was training to be a private eye or something. When he started trying to help with our homework, it really did my head in.

Thank God for Granny. She wouldn't dream of trying to help us with our homework. I looked at her, laughing at Kieran as he got revved up for one of his teacher impressions.

'Right, this is Mr Mercer, OK?'

Mr Mercer is my English teacher too. He's got the broadest Scottish accent known to man.

'Failing to plan,' said Kieran in a deep voice, marching dramatically over to Granny, and eyeballing her as though she was a bad student, 'is planning to *fail*!'

I couldn't help laughing. The accent was spot on, and Kieran had latched on to old Mercy's favourite catch phrase.

Granny started spluttering. 'That's quite clever, that is,' she said, repeating it to herself. 'Hmm . . . We could all learn something from that.' Then she looked at the clock and bit her lip.

The horrible thoughts came flooding back into my brain. I couldn't get away from them.

Something bad was about to happen. I could feel it. In fact, I'd been feeling it for days. Mum was building up to some big announcement, and I reckoned I knew exactly what it was going to be. I could have pumped Granny and got it out of her, because it was obvious she was in on the big conspiracy too. But I didn't, because I dreaded finding out I was right.

'When's Mum coming back?' asked Kieran, turning on the telly. He must have caught that glance at the clock too.

'She won't be long. Then I'm going to help Eileen with her jam-making.'

'You don't have to wait for Mum to get back, Gran. I don't mind babysitting Kieran.'

'I don't need babysitting. I'm eleven years old.'

Granny ignored me and flapped her hand at the telly. 'Can we turn it down a bit?'

'Sorry, Gran,' grinned Kieran. 'I thought you'd like it loud, now you're getting a bit deaf!'

'Less of that, young man.' She frowned at

the presenter on the pop channel that Kieran had on. 'Look at her! Fancy showing all that stomach when you're on telly!'

'Ssh!' said Kieran.

'I don't know why you watch such rubbish,' said Granny. 'Do another impression, go on.'

Kieran couldn't resist it. 'OK, I'll do Mr Carter.'

This was going to be interesting. Mr Carter is the games teacher and Kieran hates games. He's not very good at running and he's pretty uncoordinated so he isn't in any of the football teams at school. I feel sorry for him because it's obvious he really wishes he was good at football.

Our dad runs the line for the boys' match on Saturday afternoons, and whenever we go over to Dad's for the weekend, he tries to get Kieran to play. But he says things like, 'Puffed out already, Kieran? You've got to be fit to be any good at football, you know! You can learn a lot from just watching closely and listening to the coach . . .' I reckon poor old Kieran thinks that if he takes Dad's advice he might magically get really good at footie and go back and impress Mr Carter with his new skills.

Kieran's impression of Mr Carter wasn't bad. 'Come on, you lot! If you don't get a wriggle on, it'll be time to come in before we've even gone out!'

Granny chuckled. 'Your favourite subject, eh?'

Kieran rolled his eyes. 'Ought to be banned,' he said, turning back to the telly.

I waited till Granny had her back to me at the sink then crossed my fingers and asked if Ben was coming over.

'Huh! When *isn't* he coming over?' said Kieran sulkily.

Granny turned round with the dishcloth in her hand. 'Don't be like that. He's lovely, Ben is.'

And bang on cue, the back door opened and in he came, smiling away.

'Hello everybody! And how are we all today?'

Kieran shot him a real evil. 'Where's Mum?'

'Hello, Ben,' said Granny pointedly, giving Kieran a *where are your manners*? look.

Ben smiled round and rubbed his hands together as though he was waiting for the lottery result to be announced and he really fancied his chances. Then he pulled up a chair next to Kieran. 'Your mum's on her way. I thought I'd just drop by and see what you're all up to.'

Kieran mumbled that he was going to his room. Unfortunately he zapped off the telly at the same time, so that left me, Ben, Granny and an embarrassing silence.

'Is it still raining, Ben?' asked Granny.

Why didn't she look out of the window?

'Drizzling a bit. What did you have for tea, Ashley?' He was giving me the kind of encouraging smile you might give a three-year-old. Here we go . . .

I put the telly back on. 'Spaghetti.'

'Really! Do you know, when I was little I used to call spaghetti "basketti"!' *How interesting*! 'I think I'll do my homework.'

He gave me a big beam. 'That's what I like to hear! Want any help?'

Granny brought a cup of tea to Ben. 'There you are, dear.'

'Cheers, Kath.'

'Word of advice, Ben,' she grinned. 'Never offer to help with homework.'

'OK, I know when I'm not wanted!'

Oh yeah? What are you doing here *then?*

I picked up my bag and followed Kieran's example.

Mum was late. I had nearly an hour to work myself up into a big temper. How dare Ben walk into our house like he owned the place and drive me and Kieran out of the kitchen. It was boring in my room, *and* cold.

So it was a relief in one way to hear the car

pull up, but in another way I wished it never would, because I was dreading Mum making any big announcements. I left it a couple of minutes, so she and Ben could get the kissing bit over, then I went down.

'Hi, Mum.'

'Hi, love.' She looked a bit grim, but it might just have been a bad day at the hospital.

I thought I'd try delaying tactics. 'I've done my homework.'

'Good. Where's Kieran?'

Uh-oh! Something tells me this is not hospital grimness. 'Upstairs.'

'Right, I'm off to Eileen's,' said Granny. 'I said I'd give her a hand with her jam.'

Mum patted Granny's arm. 'She's lucky to have you, Mum.'

Granny didn't answer but a look passed between them as she went to call 'bye to Kieran upstairs.

'I'm off now, love! See you later.'

''Bye, Gran,' came the faint reply.

Ben drained his cup. 'I'll walk you to the corner, Kath. I want to get a bottle of wine from the shop.'

And there it was again – that same look. They must think I'm blind or stupid.

'Ashley, can you tell Kieran to come down, please?' Mum's voice sent a chill through me. 'I want a word with you both . . .'

Collect the links in the step-chain . . .

 1. To see her dad, Sarah has to stay with the woman who wrecked her family. Will she do it? Find out in *One Mum Too Many!*

 2. Ollie thinks a holiday with girls will be a nightmare. And it is, because he's fallen for his stepsister. Can it get any worse? Find out in *You Can't Fancy Your Stepsister*

 3. Lissie's half-sister is a spoilt brat, but her mum thinks she's adorable. Can Lissie make her see what's really going on? Find out in *She's No Angel*

4. Becca's mum describes her boyfriend's daughter as perfect in every way. Can Becca bear to meet her? Find out in *Too Good To Be True*

 5. Ed's stepsisters are getting seriously on his nerves. Should he go and live with his mum? Find out in *Get Me Out Of Here*

 6. Hannah and Rachel are stepsisters. They're also best friends. What will happen to them if their parents split up? Find out in *Parents Behaving Badly*

 7. When Bethany discovers the truth about Robby, she knows her family will go ballistic. Is it possible to keep his secret from them? Find out in *Don't Tell Mum*

8. Ryan's life is made hell by his bullying stepbrother. Has he got the guts to stand up for himself? Find out in *Losing My Identity*

10. Ashley can't stand her mum's interfering boyfriend. But it's possible she's got him all wrong. Has she? Find out in *Healing The Pain*